WICKED ENDS

A COLLEGE BULLY ROMANCE

HIDDEN VALLEY ELITE SERIES
BOOK EIGHT

ISLA VAUGHN

ARROWSCOPE PRESS, LLC

CHAPTER ONE

WINTER

Palms flat on the dirty windowpane, I was frozen, transfixed by the two little girls on the dock. Puffy gray clouds hung low in the sky, and I could almost feel the slight bite of the breeze as it lifted their long strawberry-blond hair, making the strands dance in the wind. Too thin and long-limbed, they awkwardly tossed pebbles into the water. I could predict each movement as if it were my own. The tilt of the taller one's head and the way they stood close to each other spoke to something missing inside me.

Seeing them felt like a cleaver to my chest, tearing and shredding me until I bled out on the dusty wooden floor. *I know them.*

The dingy window allowed for a small view, and I desperately wanted to see more of the landscape. I couldn't. *And is anyone else there?* It felt like there was, and it made me crazy that I couldn't spot anyone. The hairs on the back of my neck and along my arms stood from some strange static or electrical current that charged the air. Or maybe it was the sense of doom I couldn't shake.

It's not safe repeated in my head, rising in volume, the rhythm merging with that of my palm striking the glass, warning them. *It's not safe.*

The dock was old, and I swore I heard the creaks as they moved along the edge, playing a game of who could throw the small stones the farthest.

I didn't like how close they were to the edge. Panic clawed at my throat, making it difficult to yell, but I tried to caution them. I couldn't shake the ominous feeling that they were in danger.

My vision tunneled. I pounded my fists on the glass, screaming for them to get away from the water. To run. I had to get out there. I tore my gaze from the girls and searched the room, finding a single bed, one window, and no door. *How can there be no door?*

Someone was coming. I could feel it in my bones. I beat against the glass pane with renewed effort, shocked it didn't break. My heart pounded with a sense of urgency, and my hands shook. *I know what'll happen.* I screamed as loud as I could for them to run.

They can't swim.

Sweat beaded along my hairline and rolled down my face. It was going to happen. I could almost hear the sound of a footfall. I backed up and threw my body against the window only to bounce off, landing on the floor. There had to be a way to get free. I picked myself up and repeatedly hurtled my body at the wall until the room's edges expanded. It brought me closer to the dock.

Then I heard it—the creak of the old, rickety dock under my feet.

I couldn't understand. A wall had never moved like that before. When I thought about it, I was snapped back into the room as if nothing had changed.

It's a dream. Acute fear spread through me like wildfire. I didn't want to relive it because I knew—one of those girls was me.

The wood creaked again. Pain exploded along my back, knocking me off the dock. The next moment, I was underwater. I kicked and flailed my arms, the surface there then gone. Blind fear added weight to the water. My limbs grew heavier. I held my breath as long as I could, then I didn't. It was involuntary. I had no control over the quick intake of water. It went down my throat and into my lungs. Everything was heavy. Pressure surrounded me.

I couldn't fight it.

I woke with a gasp, air filling my lungs. My body remained heavy, and my mind felt hazy like I was underwater. Crickets chirped outside, and moonlight cast a silvery glow through a window. I blinked the room into focus, but it only managed to add confusion.

Where am I? Faint light filtered through a window coated with grime. It was enough to make out dated wood paneling on the walls. Nothing was familiar. A damp mustiness clung to the air. Dust infiltrated my every breath. The tiny particles tickled the back of my throat, and I coughed. My heart pounded in my chest at the noise.

Did I alert someone I'm awake?

The violent beat of my heart matched the one in my head. Bile climbed up my throat, and my vision swam. Dark spots converged on the edges of my blurry vision as more information trickled in. I lay acclimating to my surroundings.

I wasn't in my dorm room at Thane University.

I tried to sit up, but I couldn't move my arms. The nausea increased, my stomach cramping painfully. Then I felt the bite of plastic on my skin, securing my hands behind me, and a new wave of panic sent racking tremors through my weak limbs. I fell back on the bed, the rough sheets scratching under my exposed skin.

My ears strained for sounds in the rest of the house. There were none, just the faint lapping of water coming from somewhere outside. I tried to swallow past the Sahara that was my mouth, but it did little to relieve my urge to throw up as my stomach churned and my head throbbed painfully.

The dark spots united, and I knew I couldn't remain conscious much longer, despite the realization that none of it was a dream. With each measured breath, my heartbeat slowed —until I realized what had happened.

Someone had kidnapped me.

CHAPTER TWO

SHANE

Blue and red LED lights flashed with glaring brightness. I shifted, unable to find a comfortable position with my arms secured behind me, handcuffs biting into my skin. Cars slowed as they passed. I couldn't blame them. It was a goddammed spectacle. Two squad cars surrounded my SUV on the side of the highway.

I tracked the four officers talking in front of the car I was trapped in. I hated this feeling of frustration and helplessness.

What the hell are you doing, Winter? My mind warred between disgust and worry.

She's missing? The officer had told me she was. It was yesterday morning when I'd left her bed. *What could have happened between then and now?*

As I sat alone in the back of one of the cop cars, my mind spun with the events of the past few minutes. I replayed everything from when sirens whirred and blue and red surrounded me. My hands had gripped the wheel tightly as I pulled over to the highway's shoulder. They'd had me get out of the car, place my hands on the back of my head. When I'd tensed, the officer closest to me had reacted. After having me get down on the ground, he'd slapped handcuffs on me.

Only after they had me in the back of the squad car had they shown me the evidence bag they'd collected from the crime scene. My wallet had sat inside the sealed plastic, painting me as the suspect. *And for what?* They'd told me that too.

Abducting Winter Patten.

The driver's-side door opened, and the most senior of the four officers got behind the wheel. His partner followed a few seconds later on the passenger's side. He swiveled so our gazes locked. "I need to clarify that you're not under arrest. You're being brought in for questioning."

Not buying it. "Then what's with the handcuffs, and why am I in the back of a squad car?"

"Officer Myers viewed your reaction as a threat and cuffed you."

"A threat for what?" I growled, my body straining against the restraints. I had done nothing except glance at the other officers. He ignored my question as we pulled into traffic, so I went with another angle. "What you have on me isn't a good enough reason to bring me in this way."

But it was, and I knew why they'd slapped the cuffs on me. I probably looked threatening, especially since I had both height and muscle on the officer facing me.

They said nothing else as we flew along the highway, so I kept my thoughts to myself. It wouldn't do me any good to argue with them. Too soon, we took the exit, made a few turns, then parked in the lot associated with the police station. They got out. Officer Benton—I looked at his name tag when he leaned down—opened the rear door and grasped my upper arm as I got out.

We climbed familiar cement stairs to the large entrance. I'd been to the station one too many times. The heavy metal door buzzed as the lock disengaged, then we were walking inside. My gaze skimmed over the cops who followed my path through the desks. The officers looked through me with desensitized and dead eyes. The stares dripping with open suspicion, labeling me a common criminal, fueled my resolve to make whoever was responsible for my arrest pay tenfold.

I wasn't deposited in front of a desk, which surprised me. Instead, Officer Benton led me to an interrogation room.

He removed keys from his pocket. "Turn around."

I complied because I wanted the cuffs off. The clink of metal sounded as they fell from my wrists. I rubbed where the unyielding metal bracelets had bitten into my skin, easing the sting as I turned to face Benton.

"Wait here. Someone will be in to question you shortly." He yanked the door closed, locking me in.

I paced the length of the eight-by-ten room, thinking about how crazy things had gotten. I'd come face-to-face with my childhood nemesis—Winter Patten—the one who'd brought me so low when I was young that I'd thought about ending it all. We hadn't seen one another in years, and bonus, she hadn't recognized me. I couldn't resist the chance for payback and had plotted for Winter fucking Patten to fall for me. Once she did and I uncovered her darkest secrets, I would dump her and expose who she really was for all to see. That had been going well, except I'd used a fake name—Landon—and she'd found out yesterday morning, after we'd spent the night together having the best sex of my life.

My worry for her was a cancer, eating me from the inside out. *Is she okay?* I needed to know.

No answers were forthcoming, and I glared at the locked door as I pivoted and prowled toward the other end of the room only to repeat the useless exercise.

One thing after another had plagued me that year. Nothing had gone smoothly, from the summer to that very second. And that wasn't all. I couldn't help but wonder if anything from my past had connected the events leading up to this day. *Where does that leave me now?*

With another problem on an ever-growing list.

I'd barely gotten past the potential charges of involuntary manslaughter after my single punch had killed Luke Green and nearly stolen my future. Then, Joe Wrenshall, my biological father and the man who'd abandoned Mom, Phoenix, and me, wanted a second chance—I was all about those—and was trying to make amends by pressuring me to go into business with him. The only saving grace was that he had nothing to do with my arrest, or with Winter.

And to top it off, I'd made the mistake of sleeping with Professor Cindy Elian, not one of my professors but a cougar who'd proven to be a psycho stalker when I'd ended what I thought was a casual hookup.

Jealousy ruled her when it came to any female that she spotted me with. *Could she have done something to Winter?* It was a long shot, but maybe.

I dropped into one of two chairs in the room, my head falling into my hands. Frustration rolled through me with the power and strength of ominous and threatening thunder rumbling overhead. What I wouldn't give for a fight. But the underground fights were a thing of the past after killing Luke Green—*It was an accident, but that doesn't matter, does it?* He'd swung at me, and I'd returned the favor. When he'd fallen and hit his head on the corner of a cement step, our lives had changed forever. I had to live with knowing I'd killed someone, and his future had been snuffed out.

So many things were stacked against me, and I was barely holding it together.

I shoved off the chair and again paced from one length of the room to the other. With each rotation, I felt my future slipping away. Football. College. Seeing my brother's kid grow up.

But underneath it all was a strange sense of worry for the girl I wanted to hate and hated to want.

What the actual fuck had happened to Winter?

The lock disengaged audibly, and the door opened enough to let a man inside. "Shane Bennett?"

I locked eyes with a tired-looking, somewhat-older man who was not in a uniform. I waited for him to tell me who the fuck he was. His lips curved into a smirk as if he knew what I was thinking.

"I'm Detective Jaimeson." He motioned for me to have a seat, waiting until I did before he spoke. "I have a few questions."

It was messed up. I didn't like my position, and Grandad would have my ass if I said anything without a lawyer present.

I occupied one side of the table while he took the other seat. I wanted to know what was happening and why someone had set me up, because nothing else made sense.

Detective Jaimeson flipped open a folder. "Is your name Shane Bennett?"

"Yes." I saw no reason I couldn't answer that.

"You're a freshman at Thane University and a star defensive player?"

I nodded. *Where is he going with this?*

"The same Shane Bennett who struck Luke Green. A punch that resulted in his death?"

Everything in me stilled. I felt the edges of the trap he'd set start to close around me.

"Can you tell me where the girl is?"

"I don't know anything about a girl." I assumed he was talking about Winter since the cop had said my wallet had been found where she'd been taken, but I wouldn't fall into a trap. And it felt like one.

"You haven't been arrested."

My eyes snapped back to his. *Bullshit.*

"You're here for questioning."

So nice of him to straighten that out. "Then I'm free to go since they haven't charged me with anything."

"Not quite. You're a suspect, and I need answers. It's truly in your best interest to talk."

I clamped my lips shut and fought the urge to cross my arms over my chest.

"We have a witness who saw someone pick up the girl behind her dorm building. Her phone was found on the ground, along with your wallet, like she'd dropped them when she was grabbed. The man could have been your build and height, and the vehicle was a dark SUV."

That told me whoever saw the man hadn't gotten a close enough description. What they had with the witness was circumspect.

"If you have nothing to hide, answering a few questions won't hurt." Jaimeson threaded his fingers together on top of the table.

I said nothing. We sat like that for a few minutes.

"If you tell me where she is, we can make a deal."

I didn't move. I locked everything down hard so no emotion showed. It was a game, a very dangerous one, and I would not lose. "I want my lawyer present."

He sighed then retrieved a phone and handed it to me. I wanted to call Uncle Lucas, but I didn't know his number by heart. I did know Grandad's—thank God I had his number memorized. I got no privacy as I called Grandad.

"Hello?"

His deep, gruff voice sounded through the speaker, and I almost sagged in my chair, but the detective was watching.

"Grandad, I need our lawyer. A girl from school is missing, and I've been arrested."

"Brought in for questioning," the detective interjected, and I ignored him.

"They've gone too far," Grandad growled. "Don't say a goddammed word, son. I'll send the lawyer there immediately."

With no goodbyes, Grandad hung up as he always did. He had a savage side, and it was what I needed most in my situation.

I just had to hold out until the lawyer got there and sprang me from whatever trap Jaimeson was leading me into, because he'd said "someone" had taken her, not me. That my wallet was there complicated things, but he didn't say the eyewitness had seen me specifically.

Someone rapped their knuckles against the metal door. Detective Jaimeson got up and opened it a crack, listened to whatever was said, then left the room, shutting the door behind him. I waited. It wouldn't be too much longer.

The room was empty except for two chairs and the metal table bolted to the floor. The only window in the ugly tan room was the small one in the steel door. I checked behind me for a clock, but there wasn't one. I had to have been there for a few hours, making it sometime after lunch.

I leaned back in the chair and let my head fall forward for a second, my mind wandering to the call with Grandad. Authority had always surrounded him—when he spoke, in the demands he made, and in his larger-than-life presence when he entered a room. He wasn't perfect, but he was my, Phoenix's, and our mom's family.

Worry thrummed through my mind about how I was giving Joe a second chance, which would cause Grandad to blow a gasket when he found out. And he would find out. I just didn't want it to be right then.

Five minutes passed, then ten, or what I assumed was that length of time, and still, no one came to open the door and get me out of there.

The longer I sat, the angrier I got. Winter being gone reeked of a setup. My heart pounded a steady rhythm, and my body grew tense. I was the fool who'd slept with her, thinking I would wrap her around my finger and hurt her in the worst possible way when the time came, just like she'd destroyed me with bullying when we were kids. But the joke was on me because she'd one-upped the stakes and had taken things to a criminal level with her stunt.

She must have orchestrated the abduction. And when a nagging doubt that she hadn't crept into my thoughts, I stomped on it until I could no longer hear it. I could barely restrain myself from the urge to storm out of there and make her confess by whatever means necessary.

The door opened, and my lawyer, Frank Nicholson, appeared. "I'm here, Shane."

"I didn't do anything." I needed that out in the open, and I wanted him to believe me. I may have been guilty of some things, but Winter's abduction, if that was even real, wasn't one of them.

Frank shoved his hands into the pockets of his dark-blue pants, his suit crinkling around them. "The police have Winter's phone with a text message traced to a burner number with a conversation about your wallet, telling her to meet you outside and by the back."

"I don't have a burner phone, and I did not message Winter about my wallet. I didn't even realize it was missing."

"They also have an eyewitness."

Anger raced up my spine. "No one named me, because I wasn't there." I needed to think it through, and I uncurled my fists, flattening my palms on the cool metal table. Even if I hadn't told everything to the detective, I needed to with my lawyer. "I spent the night with Winter the night before last. I stayed at Mom's last night, and I was on my way back to Thane when the police picked me up. My time is accounted for. I didn't do anything to Winter."

"Good." Frank nodded, and I appreciated his calm professionalism. "Sit tight and don't say a word while I get this straightened out."

He didn't have to tell me twice. I caught a glimpse of Detective Jaimeson before the door shut. He stood to the side, his frustration evident in the frown that carved deep lines around his mouth and between his brows.

Denying I was involved didn't appear to matter, because it seemed no one at the police station believed me.

CHAPTER THREE

WINTER

I lay on my side on the musty old mattress, confused about what was real and what wasn't. My dream had been vivid and far too detailed to have imagined everything. Sweat coated my forehead, and I ran my fingers through my damp, tangled hair.

The sense of impending danger quickened my breath until it crashed against the rough, smelly pale-blue sheet I lay on. The need to run far from the water crashed through my system, chasing away a fraction of the haze in my mind. But with the adrenaline rush, the image of the two girls on the dock faded.

Summer. A tear formed in the corner of my eye before spilling down my temple. I'd seen her again. A glimpse, but it was enough to pierce the wall that blocked me from my view into the past.

With each blink of my eyes and every inhalation, the window into my psyche faded. The answers were there but elusive and slippery. I was close to understanding and remembering something essential, but the more I woke, the quicker it faded.

Rubbing my wrists, I eased the phantom ache. I wasn't tied up, even though my shoulders were sore as if I had been.

Crickets chirped, and the low-pitched croak of a tree frog filled the silence. I strained for the sound of another's presence. Only when I was sure there were no noises except for the insects and animals outside did I contemplate moving from where I lay.

My head pounded with the sluice of my blood. Each beat of my heart made my head expand until it seemed set to burst. My tongue felt thick and dry, like cottonmouth from some terrible hangover. My lips were parched, and a small split stung every time my tongue worried past it.

I blinked the dim room into better focus. The last time I'd opened my eyes, or I'd thought I had, the moon had illuminated the room. Currently, the faint glow of light was from the sun rising—*Or maybe setting? How much time has passed?*

Wood paneling covered the walls. I occupied the only furniture in the small space. I studied the window across from the foot of the bed and one in the door on the same wall, which would give me a glimpse of my location.

My gaze slowly swept the room, and I noted the other door that lacked a window. I didn't even want to attempt to go through for fear of who might be on the other side. The one with the window was my best chance at a way out.

I dragged myself into a sitting position and waited while the spinning room stabilized. I wiggled my toes and wondered where my shoes were. Not on the floor, from what I could see in the semidark room.

Slowly, I shuffled to the edge of the lumpy mattress then set both feet on the floor. Taking a deep breath, I stood. I didn't dare take a step for fear of face-planting. So I remained vertical, swaying slightly on legs that trembled. Another second or two and the vertigo lessened.

I crept forward, one foot in front of the other. At the

window, I tried to peer out, but a thick coating of dust and grime made it impossible to see. A lock sat at the top of the window, and I wrestled it open. When I got it turned, I pushed against the window frame, grunting against its immobility. Putting more effort into it, I shoved with all my might. It didn't move an inch.

Maybe I can break it? Hands curled into fists, I beat against the glass, screaming for help simultaneously. I didn't know how long I did that. My throat hurt, and my voice was hoarse. I had to find something to break the window with.

Another room inspection resulted in nothing. My stomach cramped and spasmed. I dropped to my hands and knees, dry heaving. Tears spilled from my eyes and splattered against the dusty plank floor. Thoughts were hard to grasp. They moved like fleeting whispers through my mind with little substance, nothing I could capture with clarity. Except for one—I'd been drugged.

The drumbeat in my head increased to an intense, splitting throb as I crawled through the splattered tears back to the door. It took effort, but I curled my hand around the doorknob. With every ounce of strength, I twisted it and pulled. When it gave, I fell back on my heels, shock spreading through me in a tingling rush. I'd been so disoriented, I hadn't even thought to check the door. I'd assumed it would be locked.

My fingers dug into the doorframe, and I used it to stand. Then I stepped outside, and the sight that greeted me sent a jolt of fear to my heart.

I'm at McMillan Lake.

CHAPTER FOUR

SHANE

No one believed that I didn't do anything to Winter. I hadn't told the detective anything. But I had given Frank, my lawyer, my alibi. He'd come in, dropped the facts that the police had, and gone to work on getting me released. Mom would vouch for me, as would the professors for the time I was in class the day before.

But I was still in the interrogation room, waiting. It was better than a jail cell, but it didn't stop the sensation of fire ants crawling over my skin. I wanted to tear the door off the hinges and make a break for it.

My wallet. A witness. And someone took Winter. *What the fuck is going on?*

That kind of thing was rare where we came from. It didn't happen to people like me and my family. And because of Luke Green, since I knew Winter, the cops assumed I was involved in her kidnapping and, maybe, worse. I bounced my leg, not liking that it could be worse. I needed it all to go away. And I feared they wouldn't let me go until they could pin whatever had happened to Winter on me.

The door opened, and I snapped to attention as a female

detective entered, a folder in her hand. She dropped it onto the table and took the seat across from me.

A knock sounded as the detective opened her mouth to say something. She snapped it shut and stood, cracking the door to hear what the person on the other side wanted. When she turned back, her features were taut and fury heated her eyes. "I wasn't aware your lawyer is here."

Frank entered and leaned against the wall next to me. He shoved his hands in his pockets and locked his don't-fuck-with-my-client gaze on her.

"I'm Detective Carson. I was assigned to this case."

When she nodded at me, I sighed and looked down, not acknowledging her. *Why are they still talking to me?*

"Can I get you anything? Coffee? Water?"

You can get me out of here. Other than that, I wanted nothing from her. I shook my head that I didn't want anything.

"Do you consider hurting yourself?"

What the fuck? I jerked my gaze to hers, dread heavy in my gut. "No." I growled the denial in her direction.

She slid a finger under the folder's edge, flipped it open, and pulled out a worn piece of paper. My body filled with tension, and I fought against my fight-or-flight mode urging me to move, to do something, because she had my old suicide note in her hands. It had been folded and unfolded about a thousand times, worn from being in my wallet to remind me how evil Winter was.

Frank strolled to Carson's side and lifted the note from the file, his eyes skimming over the childish handwriting.

A combination of embarrassment and fury prompted me to blurt, "That was written when I was a kid. I'm not the same person anymore." Not by a long shot. I only kept it as a reminder of what could have happened and what never would.

"Do you know where Winter Patten is?"

"No."

"When was the last time you saw her?"

"Don't answer that." My lawyer's authoritative voice snapped through the room, echoing off the walls as he dropped the note back onto the table and returned to his stance leaning against the wall.

"Winter is mentioned in this note." Her eyes went soft, but it wasn't real. "She bullied you, didn't she?"

"Don't answer that," Frank barked.

It was ridiculous. I wouldn't have hurt Winter. Not physically, anyway, but they didn't need to know that qualification. It wouldn't go well for me if they did.

"Is that what happened? You had history with this girl and saw an opportunity to get even. You're not a little boy anymore, are you? You are a big strong man, and you've been carrying this note around just waiting for the opportunity to put her in her place, to show her how weak she is compared to you. Isn't than right, Shane, with your good looks and your place on the football team? Is that what happened? You got an opportunity to take revenge and took it too far?"

I froze. She pretty much had me dead to rights. I did carry that note around to remind me of what Winter had done to me all those years ago. I was looking for revenge, but not in the way she'd suggested.

"I didn't do anything to Winter. I don't know where she is, and I don't know who took her," I said over Frank telling me not to answer that.

She shot him a peeved look before resuming her sympathetic expression that I didn't buy one bit. She was trying to get me to confess, but I hadn't seen Winter since early yesterday morning, when I left her dorm room while she was sleeping. I ignored the detective's question because I saw no point in incriminating myself. They should be out looking for Winter instead of wasting my time.

"Where is Winter Patten?"

For fuck's sake. "I don't know! And instead of harassing me, why don't you go find her?"

Frank shot me an annoyed look before turning back to Detective Carson. "The way I see it, you have no evidence other than his wallet, which is circumstantial. So unless you plan to arrest him and press charges, we're leaving now."

CHAPTER FIVE

WINTER

I rested my head against the backs of my hands, willing my thoughts to make sense. Everything was fuzzy, hazy, and complicated the most straightforward task. But I was outside. Free from the cottage that someone had left me in.

And that was another problem. *How much time do I have until they return?*

I couldn't risk finding out. Palms flat against the grimy cedar outer wall, I pushed off it, standing for a second before I moved farther outside. I had no idea whose house I was in, but—*I remember it.*

The dock. Down the gently sloped yard, weathered planks formed the same dock that lived in my nightmares. Intense fear sliced into me, stealing my breath and causing me to waver unsteadily on my feet. The dull throb beating in my head grew, echoing loudly in my ears.

I couldn't look away. I'd thought the dreams weren't real, but a fresh wave of fear almost took me to my knees. *I have to get out of here.*

I hadn't been reliving what had happened in my dream. My dream had been my mind trying to warn me. Danger shimmered amidst the spots threatening my vision as I put one foot in front of the other. The apartments where I used to live with my sister and mom weren't far from there.

As I walked, I kept my head down, taking a few shortcuts where I could. My feet were a mess, but I hadn't seen my shoes anywhere when I'd woken. That was the least of my worries as I hurried to the apartment complex as fast as I could.

The position of the sun indicated it was sometime in the morning. *Maybe close to lunch?* It was hard to tell. I didn't have my phone on me.

After about a half hour, I made it to the apartment building. *Please be home.* I hurried as fast as I could up the front steps and slipped inside. The security was a joke. It always had been. My fingers curled around the railing, and I heaved myself up the stairs until I arrived on Mrs. C's floor. While I knocked, I sent a silent prayer she was home and not visiting her grandkids.

My ears strained to hear. The faint sound of the TV followed by the slow shuffle along the floor sent a rush of relief. The door swung open, and I was greeted by Mrs. C's widening dark eyes. Her pale, papery face creased in a flash of warmth that was quickly replaced by concern.

"Winter. Where are your shoes, dear?"

My lower lip quivered, and a tear escaped to roll down my cheek.

"Oh my." She grasped my arm and gently pulled me inside.

I crowded her, desperate for the comfort she'd always given so freely. She guided me to the floral couch that had seen better days. I sank into the familiar cushions, my arms wrapping around my middle.

She eased herself onto the couch and turned toward me. "Tell me what happened."

So I did. The words spilled out of my mouth, and her hand fluttered to hers with a gasp. Before I was done, she retrieved her phone, pressing it into my hands.

"You need to call the police."

She was right. I wasn't thinking clearly. I should have called the police immediately. *What if I led whoever did that to me to her?* With fingers that shook, I punched in 911. I would never forgive myself if anything happened to her.

I gave all the same information to the 911 operator, and she told me to sit tight and that a police officer would be there within the next few minutes.

After handing Mrs. C the phone, I stood. "I should go wait for them out front."

She ambled to her feet, the slight swoop to her shoulders more pronounced than the last time I'd seen her.

"Thank you for letting me in, Mrs. C."

"Estelle, dear." She looped her arm through mine. "And I'll be waiting out there with you."

I blinked back tears. I didn't want to tell her, but I wasn't keen on being in the open alone. We took the stairs at a comfortable pace for Estelle—well, for both of us. I didn't feel that great either.

On the front stoop, she lowered herself into one of the two Adirondack chairs someone had put out front. I didn't recall them being there last time, and I furrowed my brows, wondering if I'd just not noticed them.

"Ben, my son, brought these over for me to use." She patted the other seat, and I sat next to her. "You're at the university up the way? I thought that's what you told me last time you were here."

"Yes." I smiled.

"Well." She squeezed my hand before returning hers to her lap. "You'll probably find out your abduction was some terrible hazing thing with a club or sorority."

It wasn't, but I didn't want to alarm her more than I already had.

"And it's good that you showed up at my doorstep this week

instead of next."

"Why's that?"

"My son and daughter-in-law bought a new house with a mother-in-law suite. They insisted that I move in with them and their boys."

The flash of blue and red lights and the whine of a siren stopped me from answering. We both followed the path they took. A fire truck preceded the ambulance, and my fingertips tingled from a jolt of anxiety. I shielded my eyes from how blinding they were. The vehicles stopped at the end of the driveway. It was too much. I didn't want all that attention.

It wasn't long until two officers alighted from the squad car. The paramedics were hot on their heels, and I struggled to swallow past the lump in my throat.

"Winter Patten?" one of the officers asked.

"Yes." I stepped off the porch toward a man who looked about an inch taller than me and had kind eyes. Tears welled in mine at the hint of compassion. I couldn't figure out what had happened from the time I reached the back of my dorm—or where my shoes and phone were, or how I'd ended up inside that house and, worst of all, at McMillan Lake.

"I'm Officer Stevens." He produced his badge, and I pretended to look at it, my eyes still struggling to focus.

The paramedic moved in, and my gaze volleyed between them.

"Are you injured?"

"No, I don't think so." The need to escape everything and hide in my room overrode anything else. I took a moment and rushed Mrs. C—she would always be Mrs. C to me, even if she insisted on me calling her Estelle—to hug her. "I'll be okay."

"If you're sure, dear." She shifted her sharp eyes to the men who surrounded me. "You take good care of Winter, young man."

Officer Stevens's lips twitched, and his eyes sparkled. "We

will, ma'am." He waited until she ambled back inside, then the paramedic led me to the back of the ambulance and got to work taking my vitals.

Stevens followed. "If you don't mind, I need to ask you a few questions."

I nodded. The paramedic released my arm, and it fell to my side, heavy. Everything was heavy. I wanted to sink to the ground but gritted my teeth and did my best to keep my back straight and my butt planted in the ambulance as I told the officer what I remembered.

I winced. "Ow."

The guy checking me over had found a sensitive spot on the side of my head.

"You have a lump here." He gently prodded around it. "It's outward, which is better than being indented." My hair was parted in a few places as he peered at it. "No contusion."

A penlight shone into my eyes, and I followed his directions —look right, left, up, and down. He asked how many fingers he was holding up. I answered his question while my head ached. Chloroform was their guess when I recalled the rag over my nose and mouth after whoever had surprised me had slammed my head against the doorframe.

"You probably have a mild concussion, which would account for the dizziness. You should get it checked further."

"No. I'm all right." *Sort of.* I just wanted to go home and sleep. I shivered. Maybe not alone, though. I wasn't ready for that.

It wasn't long before the paramedics reluctantly cleared me to leave. Stevens recorded everything the paramedics said and also insisted I go to the hospital. I continued to refuse. I didn't need another bill hitting my foster parents. They had done so much for me as it was, and I knew I was mostly okay. A doctor couldn't do anything other than give me pain pills, and Tylenol was the strongest medicine I wanted to take. My mom's addictions had left a lasting impression on me.

I also hoped to keep everything a secret from my vacationing foster parents until I couldn't. If they learned about what had happened, they would hop on the first plane home and cut their Hawaii vacation short. I couldn't be the cause of that either.

The officer asked if I would mind showing him where I'd woken so they could set up a crime scene. My throat tightened, and when words got stuck in my throat, all I could do was nod. We drove in silence. I'd already informed him it was at McMillan Lake.

Then we arrived, and I about peed my pants. The sight of the dark-brown cottage caused bile to bubble and gurgle in my gut. I swallowed it down and sucked in measured breaths in an attempt to regain control.

I pointed to the cottage. The tremor that shook my finger wasn't something I could hide. "That one." My voice was reed-thin and squeaky.

Stevens gave the details over to dispatch, and the squad car that had parked behind us remained as we pulled away and headed to the precinct.

A Detective Carson took me aside when we arrived and told me what they knew. About the wallet and my phone being found, the texts asking me to meet out back to return a wallet, and the eyewitness to someone stuffing me into a car. Then she led me to a room.

I stopped in my tracks when I saw Shane exiting another room farther down the hall. Some neurons must've started working, because everything clicked together in that instant.

"You were arrested?" The words burst from my mouth.

"He's a suspect in your kidnapping," Detective Carson clarified.

I took a step back, the news an instant shock to my system. A rush of anger followed, and I grasped onto it. "Huh, that makes sense now that I know who you really are. Which makes it even worse since you already knew who I was." It felt wrong to say. I couldn't stop myself. I hated that in his story, I was the villain. But everything had shifted, and he'd become the bad guy in mine. "So, you did it."

"Did what?" Shane stopped in front of me, his shirt tight across his shoulders and molding to his washboard stomach.

I got momentarily distracted. Just the night before last, I'd had my lips all over him. *And now...* I shook myself free from images of sleeping with him. "Kidnapped me."

"Hardly."

"It makes perfect sense. You did it because you're the boy I used to be mean to." And I hated that.

"Bullied."

"Whatever. That barely matters since I got jumped when and where you told me to meet you." I crossed my arms over my chest and did my best to ignore the detective at my side.

"Think about that." His expression gave nothing away. Instead, his features were cold, chiseled from stone. "If I lured you downstairs to return my wallet, why would I leave it behind so the cops could find me?"

"Maybe you dropped it." But I wasn't convinced. None of it made sense. "And how would some random kidnapper know I had your wallet?"

"I didn't even know I'd lost my wallet when the police picked me up. I could've dropped it any other time. Maybe this is just another ploy of yours to humiliate me and trash my name."

"I can't believe you said that."

A bitter laugh fell from his lips. "Why not? Based on everything you did to me when we were young, this seems like something you would do."

"What are you saying?" I took half a step back before I realized what I'd done and held my ground.

"I don't believe you were kidnapped. You probably set the whole thing up. Maybe even called the tip in yourself."

What an asshole. I strode forward until I was in front of him then jabbed my finger into his hard chest. "I did not set any of this up."

He didn't move a muscle. But I felt him coiled and ready to strike. I regretted pushing him for half a second when his eyes narrowed to slits.

"You probably made sure the note was there to incriminate me further. It's a setup. When are you gonna admit it?"

"You're insane."

"Shane," growled an annoyed man in a suit who must have been Shane's lawyer as he came toward us, a bag with a wallet in his hand. "Stop talking. Let's go."

"Winter," Detective Carson interrupted. "We need your signature on some paperwork, and, Shane, you're free to go, but don't leave town."

Shane said nothing. As he brushed past me, I shivered. What I wouldn't give to go back to the night in his arms, when everything was simpler. But it wasn't, and I was simultaneously confused and furious.

After I assured the cops that I did not want to get checked out by a doctor, I left the station. But when I got outside, he was waiting for me.

Everything was horribly wrong. It was the town. I shouldn't be there. I should never have listened to the therapist and Brooke when they said I needed to face my past. Nothing but misery waited for me there.

"Did you know all along who I was?" My voice sounded hollow, even to my ears.

He froze but didn't turn his head. "Yes." He was cold, distant even. "Did you know?"

I shook my head. An unnamed emotion squeezed my heart painfully.

"I don't believe you."

My head snapped back as if he'd slapped me. "Why? I've done nothing to prove I'm distrustful. That's all you, buddy."

"You were awful to me. It got to me, Winter." He straightened from the brick pillar he was leaning against and prowled toward me, the embodiment of fury.

His note. I clasped my hands to hide the tremble of emotion that shot through me from the pain I'd brought him then. *Look at him now. He's incredible. So strong.* Nothing could harm him, and he'd kept things from me. The fact was that he knew who I was and deliberately set out to deceive me. Shoring up my defense, I slammed up walls against the past and crossed my arms over my chest. I locked my leg muscles, determined not to let him see how he affected me. "Must not have been too bad, since you fucked me."

He said nothing, which only made me want to scream at him, to get any reaction over the rejection I felt deep in my soul. Then he walked away, and I staggered back. I couldn't let it go at that.

CHAPTER SIX

SHANE

Winter was more trouble than she was worth. I'd walked away, let her have the last word. I should've gone back and detailed what every insult she'd wielded like a weapon had done to me as a kid. Made her see how dark my world had been. I hadn't.

The next morning, I headed to classes as if nothing had happened. As I left my last lecture hall, Professor Elian crossed my path and abruptly stopped.

"Shane." She rested her hand on my arm, feigning sympathy. "I'm so sorry to hear about what happened."

I stepped to the side of the building to avoid people overhearing. She followed as I knew she would. "Excuse me?"

"I was so concerned when a friend told me you were taken to the police station and questioned about that girl."

Her concern, genuine or not, only added to the anger brewing for what Winter had put me through. "It's no big deal." It was.

I wanted to get away from Cindy and find Winter to tell her what I thought of her.

"It is, though, and if you need someone to talk to, I'm here for you." She squeezed my arm and stepped closer, her floral perfume surrounding me. "I heard they found the girl."

I snorted. "Yeah, the kidnapper must've been pretty inept."

Her lips pursed, and a second passed. "Maybe whoever took her just wanted her to know they could get to her whenever they wanted."

"I don't think Winter got that message at all." I shouldn't talk to Cindy about any of it, especially when I wanted to distance myself from her. "I've gotta go." I swept past her, putting her further from my mind with each step.

I still didn't buy that someone had taken Winter. And considering what Winter remembered about me—"You're the boy I used to be mean to"—I had every right to lie to her because she'd never even apologized.

What the fuck is wrong with me? I need an apology?

She was making me lose my mind. I didn't need anything but to see Winter Patten suffer for what she did to me, and there was no place better than to get the full story about her fake abduction from the liar herself.

CHAPTER SEVEN

WINTER

I'd never felt so alone in my life. I sat on my bed, knees pulled to my chest, and fought the urge to call Brooke and James or Jaxon. I should tell them what happened. But Brooke and James were in Hawaii, and Jaxon was spending a few days with Max's family. I just couldn't interrupt everything with a crisis. And at nineteen, I wasn't legally bound to, which didn't mean anything—*They're family*. They would want to know. For the time being, I said nothing because I didn't want to bring more trouble to their doorstep. They would circle the wagons, and part of me wanted that more than anything.

But that's not why I'm here.

I had to figure things out—both known and hidden.

Everything was a mess. I glanced at Piper's bed, noting she hadn't slept in it last night. More and more, she'd been staying at her boyfriend's place. We were just roommates anyway, and I didn't miss her being around, but it would have been nice to talk to someone who wouldn't rush in and try to save me as my foster family would.

I'm doing the right thing, aren't I? I couldn't figure it out. Between being drugged and taken to McMillan Lake and figuring out my past, which was coming back in bits and pieces, I was a complete mess.

A knock sounded on my door, and I jerked back, my head hitting the wall with a thump and propelling the constant ache into a violent throb. My heart kicked into overdrive, and my hands trembled. I scooted to the edge of the bed, dropped my feet to the floor, and once I was steady, made myself cross the room to open it.

"Who is it?"

"Shane."

I yanked the door open, bracing myself. He was the last person I'd expected. I took a step back, hand still tight on the wide-open door. I couldn't shake the panic that had gripped me since he'd knocked.

His arm brushed against mine as he pushed past me into my room. A wave of lust hit me hard, and I sucked in a breath. A vision of our night together slid into my mind like a lover's caress—my fingers buried in his hair and every nerve ending hypersensitive. I clamped my thighs together, struggling to dispel the vision of him holding my nipple between his lips with a mischievous grin.

After pushing out a loaded breath, I followed him back into my room, the door slipping through my grasp. It shut with a decisive click.

"What do you want?" *And why am I still affected by him?* He was a liar and possibly the one who drugged and kidnapped me.

He turned and faced me, his feet shoulder-width apart and arms crossed over his impressive chest. The room seemed to shrink with him in it, and I moved so my back was to the door, increasing the distance between us. Desire simmered in the air between us. Or maybe I was the only one affected. I bet I was. And that did the trick. I pushed some of the lust-filled haze from my eyes and glared instead.

"I wanted to make sure you're okay."

Yeah, not buying it. He had an edge that said otherwise. "I'm fine, but I want to know why you lied to me."

He shrugged. "I was embarrassed."

No elaboration. No apology. I called bullshit on that one. I narrowed my eyes and mirrored his pose. I wouldn't say a word until he did.

"Look, I didn't kidnap you. What possible reason would I have to do something crazy like that? Especially after we spent the night together." His arms fell to his sides, probably in an attempt to come across as less defensive. "I came here to check in on you. That's it."

The heaviness in the air between us said there was more to it. "Well, you've done that."

I should apologize. *Right?* In my heart, I didn't think he was the one who took me. Even though I had been so angry with him when I saw him at the police station. My gut said he wasn't guilty, not about that. But the problem was things weren't adding up, and that was why I held back from apologizing for accusing him. So many coincidences—I should pay attention to those.

"What happened? When I left your room for class that day, you were still asleep."

I hesitated because he sounded off, but maybe that was due to being arrested. I didn't know anymore. "Someone jumped me from behind. They slammed my head against the doorframe then put a rag over my mouth—"

"Did you tell the police about that part?"

"Yeah. They think it was chloroform because it was sweet smelling. They found no traces of it, so they couldn't do anything about it." I was still confused, foggy. My mind was sluggish, and I hoped I'd gotten all the details correct.

"Did you lose consciousness?"

"I did." *Why am I telling him this?* I worried my lower lip with my teeth, wrestling with what to do. There was no argument—I needed to talk to someone, and other than my family, I felt closest to him. "The last thing I remember before that was opening the rear door to the building to meet you and give you back your wallet. When I came to, I was lying on a crappy bed in an old cabin."

"Was anyone else there?"

I shook my head, and my stomach churned. "It was so weird. I wasn't tied up, and the door was unlocked. What was the point of taking me?" But a part of me knew. It was to remind me of what had happened when I was young and maybe to send a message that it could happen again.

Or did it have to do with my mom's parole hearing?

I wanted to confide in Shane because, despite how messed up our relationship was, something drew me to him. Maybe it was our pasts connecting us in a way I hadn't experienced in a long time. But I needed to remember he wasn't my friend. He'd concealed his identity and slept with me. That was all kinds of messed up, but clearly, so was I.

Another knock vibrated through the door and into my back, and I jumped about a foot. I had to get a handle on my nerves. I was in my dorm room. I was safe there. When I opened it, Mark, my RA, stood there.

"Hey, Winter. Are you okay? I heard what happened."

"Yeah, I'm… fine."

"Look, I'm sorry to bother you, but I need you to fill out a form about the back door incident."

"I thought I already did that with campus security."

Mark shrugged, looking bored with the conversation. "I don't know. The housing director said you need to come to the office and told me to bring you there. It'll take a couple of minutes."

"Oh, okay." I glanced at Shane then decided not to worry about him. We could pick up the conversation when I got back.

I went with Mark to the housing office and filled out the

form about how I'd opened the back door and someone had come from behind me. The housing director told me it was so they could get a camera put on the door from the inside also. We chatted for a few minutes, then I left. When I returned to my room, Shane was gone.

CHAPTER EIGHT

SHANE

Alone in Winter's room while she filled out a form for the housing director, I weighed my options. My life had been a series of moments that had shaped me, decisions made, good and bad, that had turned me into who I was. Turned out—thanks to an untied shoelace—I was a thief.

The shoe was at fault, really. Had it not been untied, I never would've bent to fix it and pulled the lace hard enough to break it. My hand hit the shoebox under Winter's bed, and it moved too easily to contain a pair of shoes. Everyone knew the importance of a hidden shoebox. Both my brother and I had them, and Mom probably did too.

I flipped the lid and stole a peek, finding a whole lot of temptation.

It was a chance I couldn't pass up. With the shoebox under my arm, I left Winter's room and returned to the football house. Once in my room, I opened it. It held stacks of bound letters addressed to Winter, with the return address from the Central California Women's Facility, inmate number 1987078, Patten, Katrina L.

The letters were bunched in groups of twelve. I thumbed

through them and found that they were sorted by year. On the top was a letter from the parole board. It seemed like a good place to begin, and I pulled it out of the already-opened envelope just as my brother barged in.

I shoved the letter back in and slid the shoebox behind me. "What the hell, man? This isn't your room anymore."

We'd shared a room last semester before he'd moved into married housing with Aspen.

Phoenix stopped in the middle of the room, his silver eyes seeing way too much. I never could hide anything from my twin.

"I'm gonna let slide whatever that's about because we have bigger things to discuss."

"Like what?" I didn't need to ask. He knew what'd happened. I doubted Grandad had told him, but maybe.

"I heard a rumor that you were arrested again. What the hell is that about? Kidnapping? Tell me it's bullshit."

"It was a misunderstanding. They didn't arrest me, just brought me in for questioning."

"What happened?"

I couldn't lie to my brother, not about that. So I told him—everything. From running into Winter and the lie I told her about my name to sleeping with her before being pulled over and brought in for questioning.

Phoenix blew out a breath and ran his fingers through his hair. "Look, I won't disagree with your plans for Winter. That chick was downright evil when we were young. But what's the deal with her being kidnapped? You think she made that shit up?"

"I did." *Do I still?* "I don't know. I want to say it's all on her, and I'm really leaning that way, but then she mentioned something about being drugged."

"Did they send her to the hospital to get labs drawn?"

"You'd think, right? But no. Maybe she refused to go to the hospital."

"That's pretty suspect. My bet is she's making it up."

I nodded. Phoenix had been there when she'd bullied me for stuttering, among other things. He knew how much of a toll it'd taken on me, on us, because we were connected in ways other siblings weren't. When he struggled, I felt it, and vice versa. I had last semester, but I was distracted with Joe trying to come back into our lives. I'd kept that from Phoenix as long as I could. And after what'd happened when they'd met the night of his last fight, then after, I wished I'd never brought him to Joe's hotel.

"I also stopped by because we need to head to Mom's tonight for dinner."

"Why? And is Aspen coming?"

"Not this time, bro. She doesn't know about your trip to the police station yet. I'll tell her after we handle Mom's freak-out."

Goddammit. Winter caused me so many problems. I should stay far away from her and give up on the revenge plan. But it wasn't easy, and I couldn't quit her.

"We're taking your car," Phoenix said, breaking into my thoughts.

I nodded, got up, and followed him out of the football house and to my SUV. If I drove, Phoenix could leave his vehicle for Aspen if she needed it since her car was unreliable.

"Are you getting nervous?"

We got in, and I pointed us in the direction of home.

"For the baby? Yeah, and Aspen is just done. She says these last weeks of the pregnancy have been tough. She doesn't sleep well, and it's been a challenge with school and her business."

"Can I do anything?" I felt like shit. My twin brother and his wife were having a baby, and I'd barely seen them lately. I'd been so caught up in balancing Joe, the nightmare concerning Luke Green, and Winter that I hadn't given them much thought.

"You've got enough on your plate right now." Phoenix stretched his legs as far as they would go in the passenger seat. "Besides, Riley, Sky, Max, and Jaxon are always over. She's not alone often if anything should happen with the baby coming early."

Max was Aspen's best friend and business partner. I took the ramp onto the highway and merged into the far-right lane.

"I'm blanking on this, but you're aware of who Max's boyfriend is tied to, right?"

"I'm not following."

"Max is dating Jaxon, Winter's brother."

"I'm aware now."

It was strange how interconnected my life was with Winter's. If I hadn't spotted her behind the counter when I'd gone for coffee with some of the guys, I was sure I would've heard about Winter from Aspen or my brother when he figured out who Jaxon considered his sister.

"It's weird. Have you met Jaxon?"

Phoenix was keeping the conversation fairly surface level, but I could feel him gearing up for the stuff he wanted to discuss without Mom present.

"We haven't met," I said.

"I'm sure you will if you continue to see Winter." Phoenix changed the radio station.

I grunted in response.

"Is it only revenge?"

I shrugged. It was more complicated than that, and I knew my brother understood without me saying the words.

"If you need anything…"

"Yeah, I know—'just ask.' Thanks." I took a minute then unloaded my biggest concern. It was better to do that with just the two of us. He was right to do our talk in the car so we didn't add to Mom's worries. "I won't ask, though. I can handle things on my own. You've been through too much since last semester."

"You know I'm fine. There are no more concerns with the

brain injury. Or not really. I'm doing all the follow-up appointments, and everything has been good."

"Do you have any idea what it was like—"

"Firsthand, bro. What do you think it was like for me to know that you were so close to taking your life because that bitch, Winter, was tormenting you? And nothing I did to stop her had any effect. It was like threatening a mannequin. The words I said to her didn't even register. But that doesn't matter. I could have lost you."

The anguish in his voice hit me hard. "I know." I would never forget what had happened to my brother when I'd insisted that he talk with Joe last semester. "I felt just as helpless when you collapsed in that hotel room during the meeting I arranged with Joe."

"I'm just afraid that—"

"I'll contemplate taking my life?"

"Yeah," he choked out, his voice rough and filled with emotion.

"It won't happen again. I'm not the same person I was when I wrote that note." I wouldn't let anyone bring me to that level of despair again, where I felt like I had nowhere to turn. Since that point, I'd grown and learned that no one could make me feel inferior unless I allowed them to, and I had no intention of letting myself sink low enough to think about taking my life again. "You know who I am, how I deal with things."

The miles dissolved too quickly under my tires. I took the exit ramp off the highway toward Mom's house.

"Okay. I believe you." A fraction of the tension in his shoulders eased. "Back to Joe. Is he still trying to be a part of your life? Because there is no fucking way he's invited into mine, and I guarantee Mom and Grandad feel the same."

He spoke the truth on that. Mom had been skeptical when she'd heard what he'd pulled. She'd said Joe had made his decision and she had no room in her life for him but we could make our own choices since he was our father—by DNA only. She'd made that last part clear. And she was right. He hadn't been a father to us in any other way. We'd never even met him until last semester.

"I haven't heard from him recently." But I would and soon. I hated to lie, but it just wasn't something I thought my brother needed to deal with.

"I don't like that you're talking to him. If you need me..."

I nodded. I could always count on my brother. "It doesn't need to be said. I was the one who let you down. You've never done that to me."

He laughed. "You know that isn't true. I told Tracey the lie about your career-ending injury so she would break up with you."

I grinned about that for the first time. "It was bound to happen. I heard you and our cousins bitching about her all the time. I stayed with her because she helped me work through a lot of the damage I experienced because I stuttered in elementary school. She helped in a way you and our cousins couldn't. When we first started hooking up, being with Tracey dissolved some of the carnage Winter had inflicted, and my confidence grew to where I didn't doubt myself anymore." I pulled into Mom's driveway, put the SUV in park, and turned it off. "Tracey had her faults, but she's not horrible."

Phoenix snorted, but he dropped the subject as we exited the car. I braced myself for the impending difficult discussion because Mom would dive deep, and I couldn't deflect the conversation from how I'd been taken into the police station. She didn't deserve that after all she'd been through with Phoenix and me that year alone.

I used my key, and we walked in. "Hey, Mom. We're here."

"In the kitchen," she answered.

Phoenix led the way while I trailed behind, attempting to wipe any leftover emotion from my features before Mom saw.

"Hi, boys." She gave us a wide smile and pulled me into a hug, which I returned for longer than normal. Then she moved on to Phoenix.

When she released him, I studied how tired she looked. It wasn't uncommon to see half circles darkening the skin beneath her deep-blue eyes or to find her hair on top of her head in a messy bun, but something else, a spark or energy about her, seemed different in a good way.

"I made pot roast. You brought your appetites, right?"

Phoenix snorted. "When haven't we?"

Laughter spilled from her lips before she ordered us around the kitchen to get the table set and to help her bring out the food. The smell of fresh bread almost had me drooling. We sat down, passed the food, and piled plates high before we attempted to speak. She knew the way to butter us up was through our stomachs. We managed a couple of bites before she started in on us, me mainly.

"I talked with your grandad—you should have told me yourself." Her eyes narrowed to slits, but it didn't conceal the hurt within them. "He told me you were involved in some mess involving Winter Patten. Care to explain?"

I put my fork on the plate and swallowed what had been a delicious bite but was suddenly tasteless as it went down my throat. "It was a misunderstanding, and I'm sorry for not calling you. I didn't want you to worry." I glanced at my brother, but he was no help as he kept shoveling food in his face.

I repeated what I knew about my wallet, the text, and how Winter had been "taken" from behind her building and dumped somewhere else. "I didn't do it."

"That's not even a question," Mom snapped. She was our fiercest defender. When she was in protector mode, no one messed with her.

"It'll get cleared up," I tried to reassure her. "Grandad's lawyer came."

"You need to stay away from that girl, Shane." Mom gave me that look that made us sit up and take notice. "She was trouble when you were younger, and she still is."

I don't know why, but that bothered me. I wanted to defend Winter. *What the fuck is that about?* I hated her. *Don't I?*

I chose not to respond, just gave a sharp nod, though I wasn't sure I could make myself stay away from Winter. I hated lying to Mom. But the nod was enough, apparently, because she shifted to Phoenix and peppered him with questions about how Aspen was doing.

"What's going on with you, Mom?" I changed the subject when she took a breath. "You seem different."

"Yeah." Phoenix set down his fork and leaned back in his chair. "You do."

Mom blushed, and my mouth fell open. "Is this about a guy?"

She was gorgeous, but not once had she dated anyone while we were growing up. It wasn't like she'd had time. I hoped I was right and she was letting herself have a life, finally.

"Holy shit. It is about a guy."

"Phoenix. Watch your mouth." Mom laughed, her reprimand losing its power. "Yes, I am dating someone. I met him at the hospital, and we've gone out a few times."

"What's his name? Does he treat you right? Because Phoenix and I'll have to kick his ass if he doesn't."

"He's wonderful. His name is Dr. Steven Matthews."

"Gross, Mom." Phoenix grimaced. "Dr. Matthews was my doc, and he's, like, a hundred years old."

"He is not, but I'm not dating him. It's his son."

"Ick. I'm not sure that's better. But… if you're happy."

He looked like he'd swallowed something sour, and I laughed.

We drilled Mom for information on her dates, and I knew, when we had time, we would do a search on the guy and make sure we couldn't find any dirt on him, because if we could, my brother and I would be paying him a visit.

It was nice having the three of us sit down to eat together. We stayed another hour after dinner. And even though Mom had summoned us home to question me, I was glad I'd come.

By the time Phoenix and I were in my SUV and heading back to Thane, I had to work hard not to speed. The letters from Winter's mom were waiting for me in my room, and I wanted to dive into them.

"Where's your head at with football?" Phoenix shifted in his seat, leaning partially against the window to face me. "I haven't seen you watch tape in way too long, and do you even do the sprints and running we're supposed to do?"

"I lift weights." *Christ.* My brother had always been a taskmaster when it came to football. I'd never had the same drive. I loved it, but I wasn't as dedicated as he was.

"That's not enough, and you know it."

I said nothing. I did know it, but I'd let my life get in the way. I had to make ends meet with the difference between my scholarship and Phoenix's full ride. I couldn't do the underground fights anymore, and my bodyguard job had ended with Luke Green's death. The only good thing was Grandad had stopped hounding me to do unpaid-intern-type tasks for his business.

"Do you still want to get drafted into the NFL?"

Do I? I thought about it for a minute. I loved the game. And though I wasn't a workhorse like my brother, I was damn good at it. "Yeah, I think I do."

"Then watch tape with me. Go on some of the runs and do the sprints."

I missed my brother. And his offer included more than just working out. It was time together. "Thanks, man. I'll take you up on that."

"Good. We start tomorrow. Five a.m."

Fuck.

"Are you still thinking of entering the draft next year?" We would be sophomores, so it would be an ambitious move, but if anyone could make it, Phoenix would.

"Nah, junior year. This year wasn't my best to get noticed with everything that happened."

"You and me both."

"Cole will go at the same time since he'll be a senior." Our cousin was a year older. His brother, Damon, was our age. "What about you? Will you finish your degree or enter the draft with me?"

"I'll wait for my senior year and enter it with Damon."

We talked football for the remainder of the drive, and when I got back to the football house and my room, relief washed over me to see the shoebox of letters sitting on my bed where I'd left it.

I hadn't decided what to do with it, but it could prove to be an effective weapon, should I choose to use it.

CHAPTER NINE

WINTER

Two days passed without seeing Shane. In that time, the uncomfortable sensation that someone was watching me intensified, but when I looked around, I saw no one. After I'd been jumped and taken against my will, it scared me out of my mind. I was careful to always leave through the front door of my building and didn't veer off common paths or away from where other students walked.

I hiked my messenger bag higher on my shoulder, found a spot on the quad's grass a good distance from a few other groups, and waited for Jaxon to meet me. I was early, so I got comfortable and pulled out my sketchbook to occupy my mind. With the sun warming my skin, I got lost in my drawing.

As I flipped the page to start a new sketch, a shadow fell over me.

"I'm furious with you." Jaxon dropped his bag beside me and sat. "I heard a rumor about someone grabbing you from the back of your building."

I met his gaze and squared my shoulders against the equal parts worry and anger swirling in his hazel eyes. "Furious" was code for "terrified." I read him, but that didn't change how prickly I felt. "I'm fine. I promise. And that's why I wanted to get together today, so I could tell you."

"Why didn't you call me immediately? Or Mom? Seriously, Winter. We're your family, and you're shutting us out. That's not right."

"I know. I'm sorry." I lowered my sketchpad and told him everything that had happened. "It's just that Brooke and James never get to take vacations by themselves, and they're in Hawaii. You know they would've flown back if I called." I poked him in the chest. "Don't tell them. I want them to have this. I'll come clean when they're home. I promise."

"I don't like it." He grunted. "Do you have any idea what it was like to hear through Thane's grapevine that you were in danger?" Jaxon's eyes grew suspiciously misty.

"I—"

"I mean it, Winter. I love you. So do our parents. And yeah, okay, I sort of understand why you didn't want to call them from the police station. But you still should have called me."

I rolled my eyes. "Um, same thing. You were with Max, meeting his parents for the first time. I was not going to ruin that." I gentled my voice. "This is the first guy you've been serious about—ever. It means something to me too. I want you to be happy. What do you think his parents would have thought if I'd called you hysterical and a total mess?"

"That my sister needed help. They would have understood if I'd rushed off to be with you. There's no excuse for not calling me. I was nearby. I would have come. I would've *wanted to come*. You can't push us away when things get hard. That's what family is for when times are tough or majorly crappy—you lean on each other."

Every truth slammed into me like a verbal punch accompanied by a mountain of guilt. "You're right. I do that. It's a constant struggle not to fold into myself when things are bad. I used to have Summer—"

"I know." His voice softened, and he grabbed my hand, giving it a reassuring squeeze. "But you have me, and I'm not going anywhere."

The fight left me, and I launched myself at him. His huge arms came around me, and we clung to each other.

"I'm sorry. I've been a mess lately, and everything's out of control."

He released me when I pulled back to sit facing him, crossing my legs.

"Wait"—Jaxon's brows furrowed—"I thought you said you were seeing some guy named Landon. Did you at least call him?"

I wrapped a blade of grass around my finger and tugged it until it came loose. I'd forgotten to bring a blanket for us to sit on. "Yeah, about that… Landon lied to me about his name."

"What? That's strange." Jaxon's brows climbed his forehead. "I have questions."

A laugh escaped me in a puff of air. I missed the easy camaraderie we had. It was different from me and my sister, or what we had after Dad died. Our lives had been about survival. With Jaxon, things were normal, the way it should be with a close sibling.

"Backing up before the lie." Warmth climbed my neck and settled into my cheeks. "I slept with him."

He scowled. "I kind of figured, and judging by the look on your face, you don't regret that part. So who is he, and why did he lie? Is there another girlfriend? And how did you find out his real name?"

"No, there isn't another girlfriend." If there were, I would have unleashed my brother on Shane after I outed him. "I hate to say that I sort of get why he lied, but that doesn't make it right." *The big jerk.* "We knew each other before I came to live with you guys, smack-dab in that time period where my world was one giant nightmare I couldn't escape. I—I took my pain out on him by bullying him."

"Winter." Jaxon's gaze narrowed. "That was then, and none of that matters anymore."

"It sort of does, but anyway"—I waved away the comment with my hand—"I found out who he really is when he left his wallet on the floor in my room the morning after. I peeked at his driver's license."

"What is his name?" Jaxon leaned forward. He was losing patience fast.

"Shane Bennett."

"Shane Bennett? Holy fuck." His head snapped back. "Phoenix's brother?"

"Twin, actually. Fraternal, of course."

Jaxon's face lost some color. "My boyfriend is best friends and business partners with Aspen, Phoenix's wife. When I run into Shane, I'll tear him to shreds."

"You'll do nothing of the sort." I was firm on that.

While I didn't think my very large brother's fight would be a physical one, he was wicked smart and could verbally slay anyone just as effectively. I'd seen it happen when I'd first come to live with my new family and some kids had tried to pick on me. After he'd finished ripping into them, they'd given me a wide berth in the hallways.

"A lot has happened between me and Shane. I don't remember everything I did to him when I was younger because of the headspace I was in, but we need to discuss whatever happened without anyone interfering. And then he was brought into the police station for questioning about my abduction—"

"Wait, what?" Jaxon cut in, shocked.

"I know, but we talked. He brought up a valid point about how stupid it would be to leave his wallet as evidence if he was the one to abduct me."

"You don't think it was him?" Jaxon frowned. "So who, then? Could it have been your roommate?"

"I don't think Piper could have, because she wasn't there that night or the next morning when I found it. But Shane's right. It would've been ridiculous to leave evidence behind where he took me."

"This is crazy." Jaxon's finger tapped against his leg. "We're missing something. Who else could've possibly set you up?"

"Yeah, I don't know. I just have this gut feeling it wasn't him." I couldn't believe I was defending Shane, but he wasn't the only one at fault. And I was a different person than I used to be. He deserved a chance to explain without our tempers getting in the way.

"I'm not cool with it, Winter. And that doesn't give you an excuse to shut me out. You're my sister. So don't try to take that from me."

I closed my eyes briefly against the pain of what his words meant. They reminded me of how I'd lost my real sister. But that wasn't it. I had a family that loved me unconditionally, a gift I'd never expected, and I was treating them like they didn't matter.

"You're right." He was bringing it up again because I'd hurt him, even though it wasn't intentional. "I'm so sorry, Jaxon. I'll do better." And I already had a way in mind to do that.

He pulled me in for another hug, and I squeezed him back just as hard. What he'd said was right. He was a real brother to me, and I needed to stop acting like he wasn't. "I want to show you something."

I untangled myself from his arms and grabbed my sketchbook, flipping back to the page I'd drawn so he could see it. "When I was out of it at the lake house, I had these vivid hallucinations"—sort of—"about two girls on the dock. But none of it was imagined. It was a memory. This is me"—I tapped the girl on the left—"and this was my sister."

Jaxon took the notebook from me and studied it, a frown marring his face. "It's from the day she died, isn't it?"

"Yes." He'd taken note of the emotion, the impending doom. I'd added to the seemingly innocent picture with several dark lines of my charcoal pencil. "I wanted to draw everything from the nightmare I had and see if I could figure out if I've missed something in my memory."

"Sort of a memory purge. It's a good idea."

I knew he would agree, and I smiled, the tension in my back melting.

Jaxon was the one who had helped me the most when he'd taught me to draw that first year. It had unlocked something inside me that was better than any therapy Brooke had taken me to. It also reaffirmed, even currently, that he was more real brother than foster. It was a treasured activity I did with him, never realizing it would turn into a passion I wanted to pursue as a career.

"You'll help me look for clues in the sketches?"

"Absolutely. I'll work on homework until you're ready to lay them out. Then we can study them for clues you couldn't remember before."

We drew together for hours in silence, the sun's rays pleasantly warming us against the slight chill in the air. Clouds moved in, but we had time before they were overhead.

My pencil moved furiously across the pages. After finishing one image, I ruthlessly flipped to a blank page, emptying my mind of everything I remembered in the dream. It wasn't until Jaxon swore behind me that I realized he'd stopped painting.

Tears ran unchecked down my face.

Jaxon ran his thumb under my eye, wiping some away. "You okay?"

I released a stuttering breath. "Just emotionally exhausted. I'm good. Promise," I reassured him as I laid all the sketches out in front of us.

He studied me for another moment. I swiped at the tears, got myself under control a little more, and gave him a small smile before he let it go. Then we bent our heads together, searching for details of anything that could hint at the memories I'd suppressed.

The past was merging with the present, and I was terrified of what it would reveal.

I thought someone pushed us in, but was I wrong? Did I lose my balance and fall, grabbing onto Summer and pulling her in? Is that what one of the mystery notes meant?

"Your memory jumps from you and your sister flailing in the water to this one." He tapped his finger against the view I had from where I lay on the dirt-and-pebbled shore, Summer directly in my line of sight with her unseeing eyes staring back at me. "So how did you end up here when neither of you could swim?"

"I don't know. I can't remember a large chunk of that day." I guessed my mind wasn't ready to give up all my secrets, but I could feel the darkness in the recess of my head, pushing to get out. It wouldn't be long, and I would have to face every second of the worst day of my life without the protective barrier that shielded me with blissful forgetfulness from those events.

We spent another half hour scrutinizing the images, then when I'd had enough and shoved them in my bag, we talked about the usual stuff until I felt better. I missed that, just hanging outside with him. I vowed to do more of it and not to make excuses for why I shouldn't spend time with him. Isolation wasn't why I was at Thane, and it wasn't what my family wanted for me either.

He walked me back to my dorm before he left on a date with Max, and we promised to hang out over the weekend. Though the drawing exercise hadn't yielded anything promising, I hoped that if I kept it up, my mind would give me something useful.

The mail room was on the way to the stairs, and I stopped in to check my box. There was another folded white paper. My heart rate increased as I pinched it between my fingers, not wanting to put my prints all over it. I took the stairs two at a time, and I was out of breath by the time I got to my dorm.

When I unlocked the door, it was to an empty room. Piper wasn't there, which was for the best. I didn't want to go into what had been happening. My bag slipped off my shoulder and fell to the floor with a thud. Free of its weight, I used a Kleenex to open the paper then stared in horror at the two sentences.

I hope you got the message. Next time, it won't be so easy to break free.

The typed note fell from my protected fingers to my desk. *I'm done.* I had to go to the cops. I tore through my desk drawers until I found a small box of Ziploc bags and carefully deposited the note inside. Then I dashed from my room, hurried to my car, and drove to the police station.

I maneuvered through traffic on autopilot, not noticing anything until I was parked, then walked through the front doors and asked to speak to Detective Carson. She met me at the locked door to the inner workings of the police department and let me inside. I studied her no-nonsense dark hair secured in a tight bun at her nape. She had a square face and strong jaw, not unattractive, but she downplayed her appearance with modest clothes that wouldn't draw attention. It made sense. If I were a detective or cop, I would do the same in her environment.

She held open the door to a small room, and I picked one of the uncomfortable chairs as she took the other across from me. "How can I help you, Winter?"

I withdrew the sealed Ziploc containing the note and handed it over with trembling fingers. "This was in my mailbox."

Carson's unplucked brows furrowed, and she pulled a set of

blue rubber gloves from her pocket, putting them on before she took the paper out and unfolded it. It took her no time to read the two sentences. "Do you know who this could be from?"

Frustration buzzed through me, but I restrained it, keeping my voice as even as possible. "No. I thought you could test it for fingerprints." It wasn't the first note I'd received, but since the others had called me a killer and had said, "I know what you did," I wouldn't share that information. It made me sound like I had something to hide. *Maybe,* a small part of me whispered, *you do.*

She offered me a patronizing smile, and my back stiffened. *Does she think I made the whole kidnapping thing up because of the argument Shane and I had? The one the whole precinct heard parts of?*

"I'll see what I can do." Then she stood. "Are you doing okay? Can I help you with anything else?"

The miniscule amount of concern she showed hit me like a sledgehammer. *She really doesn't believe me.* I'd almost caused Shane's suicide when we were young, and that painted me in a different light. "No, just please let me know if any information comes up. I-I don't feel safe." It was all I could do to get those words out.

I left, minus the note, and felt more frustrated and scared than when I'd arrived. I couldn't catch my breath driving back to campus. Jaxon was out with Max, and with how I felt, I knew I couldn't be alone. I was losing it. My fear was out of control. Maybe, I could hire Shane to protect me. Or at least teach me how to defend myself.

Then, if he'd sent the notes and was behind the abduction, I would figure it out quickly. If he wasn't, maybe he could help me learn who it was or keep me safe until the cops did. Because after that newest note, I knew I was in danger.

Instead of going to my dorm, I went to the football house but learned from the guy who answered the door that he wasn't there. He was at the field, doing sprints with his brother and cousins.

I couldn't go back to my room alone, so I went to the field, parked, and found my way into the stands to wait for him to finish. The day's light was enough that the floodlights weren't on, and I sat rooted to my seat while four incredibly athletic and gorgeous men ran sprints across the field then performed a series of agility exercises.

Their bodies were fine-tuned machines. Sweat glistened as their muscles shifted and bulged, adhering effortlessly to their every change of direction. When Shane came off the field, I called out to him. All four of the guys stopped, and heat rushed my face at their intensity and overwhelming presence.

He said something to the other guys, and after a minute, they left for the locker room while he stayed. I sank my teeth into my lower lip and got the courage to ask him for help despite everything.

When he moved to the railing between the stands and the walkway that led to the locker rooms, I stood and joined him. I was grateful for the distance as I made myself vulnerable, something I didn't enjoy. Wariness and guilt swam in his blue eyes before he locked the emotions down, shuttering his features until nothing came through.

I took it as a good sign and forged ahead. "I don't think you were behind what happened to me."

He grunted in response. I couldn't blame him for not being overjoyed by my declaration. It wasn't exactly an apology.

"But that means someone out there is, and I... I wondered if I could hire you to protect me or teach me to protect myself. And maybe until I'm comfortable defending myself, you could be my bodyguard or whatever you did for Erica?"

His lips firmed into a straight line, and a muscle leaped along his jaw. Seconds passed, the silence between us thick with too many emotions.

"I find it hard to understand why you want Stupid Stuttering Shane to help you."

My shoulders curled forward, and I blinked away the sudden dampness in my eyes. "I'm so sorry for everything I did to you when we were younger. To be honest—and this isn't an excuse—I barely remember any of it. We'd lost my dad. Then things were horrible with my mom, and I wasn't coping well. I probably channeled my shitty situation into making your life hell. That year, I was so miserable it affected everything and everyone around me."

He said nothing, and I forged ahead when he uncrossed his arms.

"I got a threatening note today."

His brows furrowed, and the angry muscle jumping along his jaw stopped.

"I took it to the cops, but I don't think they'll be any help."

"What did it say?"

"The one today said, 'I hope you got the message. Next time, it won't be so easy to break free.'"

His blue eyes narrowed. "What do you mean 'today'?"

I shrugged. "There was another one." Silence stretched between us until I gave in and told him what the other had said too. "The world is going to know you killed Summer."

"Any others?"

"Yes. I got one that said, 'Killer. I know what you did.' So, will you help me?" I waited for his decision, my entire body strung tight.

He nodded, the movement clipped and angry. "Yes. I'll help you unless you plan to accuse me of something I haven't done. Like write those notes. I didn't write them, Winter."

Christ. "I never said you had. And I'm sorry." I rushed my words, needing him to understand. "It was confusing after I'd been abducted, then the cops told me you were a suspect. I just couldn't understand what had happened or why an unknown number, which I'd assumed was you at the time, knew about your wallet. It's weird, isn't it? Who else could have known?"

"Your roommate?"

Jaxon had wondered the same thing, but that made no sense. "Piper didn't come back that night or the next morning. She had no way of knowing it was there."

We were at an impasse over what had really happened, but I didn't care. I just wanted to know that no one could get to me, and he was rock-solid. If I was perfectly honest with myself, he made me feel safe, even if he was a liar. But I could understand why he'd lied—sort of.

I pulled my long hair over my shoulder and twisted a few strands around my finger, needing something to do with my hands.

"Okay."

I sagged against the railing. "You'll help me?" A sliver of hope cut through some of the anxiety.

"Yes. And I accept your apology."

"Thank you." I furiously blinked the sudden tears away from the intense relief he'd offered. Then I flashed him a tentative smile, nervous about my next question. "Can you stay with me tonight? I'm scared to be alone after the threat I got in the mail."

A few seconds passed and I held my breath, waiting for his answer.

"Fine, but it's just me staying there to watch over you. We're not dating. Nothing's going on between us."

"Yes." I would agree to anything at that point.

"I have to shower. Meet me by the exit."

After fifteen minutes, he came out with his brother, who had a *Thane U* ball cap resting low on his head, so I couldn't see his eyes. His cousins flanked his other side, and I nervously shifted from foot to foot. But they said nothing as they walked by, leaving Shane, who stopped next to me.

I followed him in my car, stopping at a drive-through so he

could get food, then we went back to my place. Not much was said as he ate, and I did some reading for class.

When it got late, we climbed into bed together, me against the wall as he lay on my other side. The tension fully eased from me when his leg pressed against mine. The simple touch assured me I could close my eyes and he was still there.

I woke with a jolt, sensing something wrong, that someone was watching me. It was dark in the room. My palm lay flat against Shane's naked chest, his skin warm beneath it. My body was pressed against his, and his arm encircled me. We'd moved during the night, both unaware that I'd been sleeping on him while he held me.

Still, my heart jackhammered against my ribs as I waited for my eyes to adjust. When they did, I saw Piper in her bed, her head turned away from us on her pillow. Her long blond hair spilled over it and behind her as her chest rose and fell in a slow, barely noticeable rhythm. She was asleep. No one else was in the room, but I could smell the faint scent of perfume. It could be Piper's. She had about a thousand bottles of the stuff.

I should have pulled away from Shane—I doubted he would be okay with my proximity—but I didn't. I relaxed back into Shane's embrace, and yet, no matter how hard I tried, I couldn't shake the feeling that someone else had been there. I didn't sleep the rest of the night.

CHAPTER TEN

SHANE

I jolted awake, quickly cataloging the noises to determine what had woken me before sunrise. Soft snores came from my left, and I glanced at Piper's bed. Winter's roommate was back and asleep. I splayed my hand to feel Winter beside me but encountered cool sheets.

Alarm spiked through my blood, and I sat up, peering around the dark room. I spotted her sitting in bed beside me but huddled with her arms around her knees, back to the wall, tears streaming down her cheeks. She didn't utter a sound, but the expression I could make out in the moon's glow wasn't good. She looked haunted and in shock.

"Hey," I whispered. "What's going on?"

She didn't say a word. Swiping her thumb over her phone, she handed it to me. I scanned the article from *University News*, Thane's online blog, titled: "A Killer Walks Among the Students at Thane University." The social media story named Winter as her sister's killer. I skimmed most of it, getting a general idea. It went on to say that her mother was in prison for killing Summer but it was likely Katrina Patten had taken the blame to protect her daughter Winter.

Nowhere was the source noted or an interview with Katrina mentioned. *So who wrote this and why? Was it just because of the parole hearing?* I only knew about that because I'd read the official letter tucked away in the shoebox I'd stolen from under Winter's bed.

"Are you okay?"

She shook her head, the tears falling faster, and I pulled her into my arms.

Broken words fell from her lips in hushed tones. "I don't want everyone to know my mom's in prison. And I wouldn't have killed Summer. I loved her. I-I—"

"Shh." I held her tight, one hand rubbing soothing circles on her back. "No one that matters will believe the bullshit in that article. It's not a reputable site, and I doubt anyone will see it." It was gossip, though it did contain a picture of Winter. I had no idea who might have taken it or when. "Do you want to talk about what happened before your mom went to jail?"

"I can't. I don't remember. A huge hole is missing in that day. And after the gap, everything is so fuzzy I can't piece it together."

I held her, and slowly, she stopped trembling and her tears subsided. I didn't say a word, just offered comfort. My brain spun with possibilities of who might have written the article. *Was Cindy a suspect?* If she were motivated by jealousy, I could see her wanting Winter out of the picture. It was possible she'd dug up dirt on Winter to keep us apart. It wasn't hard to find information. There were articles about her sister drowning and her mom's trial.

But the threatening notes she'd gotten—they were personal. It didn't seem like something that would come from Cindy. *Is someone else out there with a grudge against Winter that runs as deep as mine?* I couldn't rule that thought out.

There was another angle parallel to what I'd toyed with for

Cindy—someone trying to keep us apart and coming at her from my end—Tracey, my ex.

Piper was friends with Tracey. I hated to think she might be involved in posting slander about Winter. *Could Tracey have roped Piper into helping?* It was a possibility.

Winter's hand fisting the back of my hair loosened as the room lightened, but she didn't let go, so I didn't either. Her body relaxed into mine until the shrill sound of an alarm cut through the peace of the moment.

Piper rolled over, her hand fumbling blindly for her phone. Once she managed to grab it, she punched at the screen with a finger to shut off the noise.

"Morning, Pipes."

"Fuck. Christ." She jumped at the sound of my voice and yanked the sheets up to her chin. "I forgot about you. Why are you here, Shane?"

"I should have told you," Winter said. "Sorry about that, Piper."

"Has Tracey been in here since Winter moved in?" I wanted to get to the bottom of what'd happened to Winter, and Piper was a good place to start, especially with her sharp mind groggy and defenseless from sleep. Something about my suspicion didn't feel right, though. Tracey hadn't been a problem since high school, and then, she'd mainly targeted Riley and Cole.

"You can't be serious." Piper flung the covers off and got out of bed, wearing sleep shorts and a T-shirt. "Why the hell does that even matter? She's definitely over you. Don't be a dick."

"Ah, there's the Piper I remember." Darkness stirred, and I fought the instinct to tear her down. The conversation I needed wasn't about anything other than uncovering who was behind messing with Winter. "Answer the question."

She heard the warning in my voice and frowned. "No. Tracey hasn't been in my room, and I've barely seen her other than on the weekends. She's been hanging out with her boyfriend whenever she isn't in class. Why? Change of heart?" A dark gleam entered her blue eyes. "It won't work. You're too late."

"Careful, Pipes. You know what I can do, along with my brother and cousins." I tightened my arm around Winter when she shifted to sit up. The issue was between Piper and me, and I didn't want her involved.

"This is college, Shane. You're not the Elite here. Thane's too big for that bullshit."

"You're forgetting. Like going to parties? We can have you banned. Have an interest in someone? A word from us can change that. And that's just a few of the things we have influence over."

We were still the Elite, seen as football gods at the top of our school—me, my brother, and my cousins—and making her life hell would be enjoyable. She made it too easy to return to that mentality. And she was wrong. Thane wasn't too big. Everyone knew who we were because of football. We were even more prominent at Thane than in high school. I laughed as the color drained from her face. She'd gotten the message.

She ran her hands down her face then let them fall at her sides. "It's too early for this. To answer your question, again, Tracey hasn't been here. She barely knows Winter exists. And why do you care?" The snark had left her voice, and her shoulders slumped.

I picked up Winter's phone, and she pressed her thumb to the access button. Then I turned it in Piper's direction with the article pulled up. She came over, took it from me, and scanned it.

"Oh no. Winter, are you okay?" She dropped the phone on the bed and reached across me, gripping Winter's arm.

I studied her while they talked in low tones. Piper seemed genuine, and I knew her well enough to recognize her tells. Eventually, Piper grabbed her stuff for the shower, promising she would sleep there or do whatever Winter needed to feel safe.

"I'll be here at night." The conviction in my voice shocked both me and them. *Why do I care? And what the hell is with the weird possessiveness roaring through me?* I didn't understand any of it, but I knew that if anyone got to mess with Winter, it would be me.

If I still want that. What the fuck is wrong with me? I should want that, but she had apologized. It'd been heartfelt, and everything I'd wanted to do to her didn't seem as important as it had before.

I didn't have time to unpack all that. It would have to wait.

When it was just me and Winter in the room, I relaxed my hold on her, and she pulled back, sitting so her back was to the wall.

"Why would you think Tracey did anything? I don't really know her."

"Because she and I dated for a few years in high school and hooked up some last semester. It was a possibility, but it doesn't sound like she would be the one to write information about your mom."

"Oh." We sat in silence, each lost in our thoughts until she crawled to the edge of her bed and pulled her messenger bag onto the mattress. "I want to show you something."

She pulled out several drawings—one of two girls standing on a dock, throwing rocks into a lake, another after they'd jumped into the water, and a third through the eyes of one girl staring at the other as they lay on the shore. Winter spread them on the bed. I knew what I was looking at. It was Winter's memory of her sister. She wasn't alive in the last drawing.

Then she pulled out one more. It was of a man with shadows around him, shaggy hair, and no visible features to recognize him by. The tone of the sketch was dark and dangerous.

"Who is that?"

"I have no idea. I've seen him in my nightmares but can never make out his face. I think he's connected to something at the lake that day. He could be a drug dealer or maybe even the detective who took me from the scene and is etched into my memory as something bad because I had to leave my sister's body behind."

Shit. That was a real possibility. "Whatever's going on, I agree that you need to be able to defend yourself."

"I have class. I would blow it off, but the professor takes attendance and I've already missed one this semester. She'll drop my grade an entire letter if I miss another."

"A professor with a power trip. Got it. I'll walk you to class, then after, we'll go to the gym, and I can teach you a few moves."

I only had two classes that day, while Winter had three in a row. After I walked her to her first one, I returned to the football house, showered, and hurried to information management. Time moved quickly, and after economics, I enlisted Damon's help. I met my cousin at the gym to explain why we needed to coach Winter.

The clang of weights intermingled with the R & B music pumping through the speakers. I returned greetings from guys I knew as I wove through the equipment until I was on the mats where Damon waited.

"What's this about?"

"When Winter wanted to talk to me yesterday, we ironed out a few things—"

"What the hell are you doing with her? Phoenix was pissed she was at the field. He reminded Cole and me who she was and what she did to you. I remember, man. So let me repeat myself, what the fuck are you doing with her?"

"It's complicated, but that's not the issue. This is." I pulled up the article on my phone and showed it to Damon. "That and then there's the fact that someone jumped her and took her off campus. So we're doing this."

Damon finished reading and handed back the phone. "You're too softhearted for your own good. But fine, I can see the bigger picture here."

Her safety. With Damon on board and promising to keep his comments to himself, I was confident we could teach Winter some key moves.

The musty smell of sweat permeated the half-full gym where I'd told her to meet us. I glanced at the clock. She should be here soon. Damon and I'd commandeered the red mat in the back right corner where people sometimes stretched. It was enough space to go through a few sparing techniques with Winter.

From the corner of my eye, I caught Davis and Ericson paused, their fingers curled around the dumbbells, arms flexed and unmoving, gazes locked onto someone who'd entered the gym. I turned and found out what, or who, rather, could interrupt their workout so easily. Winter had arrived. She must've changed after class, because she wore black leggings and a form-fitting *Thane University* T-shirt.

I lifted a hand to let her know where we were then glared at my teammates, who seemed to think she was fair game. She wasn't. I frowned because what the hell did that even mean? I was helping her, not claiming her as mine. *Or am I?* Goddamn, she confused me.

"Hey." Winter's grin faltered as her gaze swung from me to Damon.

I shoved aside thoughts I had no business entertaining. "You remember my cousin Damon, right?"

"Um, vaguely." She clasped her hands in front of her so tight that her fingers lost color.

"He agreed to help show you a few things."

She took a deep breath and untangled her fingers, dropping her hands to her sides. Her features rearranged from uncertain to openly friendly as she smiled at my stoic cousin, who didn't fully agree with me interacting with her.

"We should start with what you already know and build on that." I faced Winter on the mat, hands loose at my sides.

The corners of her lips twitched. "The extent of my self-defense comes from *Miss Congeniality*, when Sandra Bullock was on stage with her partner demonstrating SING."

Damon snorted. We'd all seen the movie at his house when his mom commandeered the TV one night. We were bored, and it was Sandra Bullock.

"Solar plexus, instep, nose, groin," I said.

Laughter filled the open space, and several heads turned in Winter's direction. I sent a few glares for good measure, ignoring how Damon's too-observant gaze bored into me.

"You've seen the movie." Winter's green eyes danced with mirth. "Good to know."

"Both, actually."

"Oh… this is fantastic." She clapped her hands together, laughing. "We'll need to do a rom-com marathon."

It was strange, but I was okay doing that with her. However, that wasn't why we were in the gym, so I pushed the prospect of a movie marathon with Winter out of my mind. "Let's get back to why we're here."

Her smile faded, and she nodded.

"We'll do something similar to what was in the movie soon. You should always try a few things before any physical contact. The first is making as much noise as possible to alert others if you're in a bad situation. Run away if possible. And if you can't easily escape, focus on all the vulnerable places: eyes, nose, throat, ears, and groin."

I motioned Damon over and moved Winter so she was to the side and could watch. "We're going to demonstrate a few moves, keeping it as simple as possible."

We reviewed examples of a strike to the nose, throat punch, different ways to crush a guy's junk, eye gouges, and boxing ears. We pulled our punches for each hit, not intending to cause harm.

After we went through a few scenarios with Damon attacking Winter in a frontward manner or from behind, we stopped. My fists were clenched from each interaction between them. I hated his hands on her, even though it meant nothing. He had Sky. No other girl caught his interest anymore. I knew that. Didn't matter —I wanted to punch him in the face anyway. I tried to detract from the jealousy tearing through me by trading places with Winter to face Damon myself and show her a few more moves.

But the best way for her to learn was by doing.

I can do this. I held onto the calm I'd gotten from demonstrating with Damon. With a clear head, I clipped out what we would do next. "He's going to come at you, and I want you to use the heel of your hand to strike up, hard, at his nose."

Damon's expression hardened, and he moved fast. Winter's eyes widened, but she thrust the heel of her hand toward his face. A soft slap sounded as Damon batted her hand away then grabbed her shoulders. Winter twisted, but he had a solid grip. Her knee came up. It wasn't fast enough. After blocking her knee, he released her and backed away.

I went over what she could've done when he executed blocks, then I let her try a few of those changes on me. Her eyes tracked my movements, and mine lingered on her curves. Each brush of my fingers against her skin heightened my awareness of how much I wanted to pull her into my arms and feel her body pressed against me, but not there. Time ticked by with agonizing slowness.

Winter learning some key moves was important. I hardened myself against the need that raged inside me with every necessary touch to align her stance and strikes and give her the best chance at escape. Muscle memory—that was what I hoped to build through repetition.

Her features were pinched, and she looked stressed, but she kept it together as we went over moves and mock attacks for the next hour. Loose strands escaped her ponytail to frame her flushed face, and her breath came in fast pants. She was gorgeous, and I was too aware of the guys nearby paying attention to her every move.

When Damon left, it was just the two of us as we walked back to her place.

"How were classes?"

She seemed to know what I meant—not the actual classes but if anyone had recognized her or said anything after the article had come out.

She shrugged. "They were okay, except for a weird run-in with one of my professors."

"Which one?"

"Professor Elian. I was excited to be in her class, but I don't know. I might drop it. She gives me a weird vibe."

She's in Cindy's class? That was a problem. "What did she say to you?"

"She said she was surprised that I would come back to this town after what my mother did—unless she didn't do it. It was weird. She must have seen the article."

Possibly, but according to my mom, Cindy knew Katrina Patten. My mood took a swan dive, not that it had been great after seeing Winter crying that morning.

I didn't tell her I'd screwed her professor. I didn't want her to know. Not that I cared what Winter thought, but Cindy might harass Winter out of jealousy, and she was crazy enough to do it. I didn't need Cindy blaming Winter or me for any disciplinary measures brought against her. And I didn't need more publicity, especially with the negativity I'd already had on my shoulders from Luke's accident and them suspecting me of taking Winter.

"Why don't you switch to Professor Potts? Aspen has a class with her and has no complaints."

"Thanks."

She smiled, and something settled in me.

"I think I'll do that."

My phone vibrated in my pocket, and I pulled it out to see who was calling. It was Joe. I hit Ignore, not wanting to deal with anything else right then. My plate was already overflowing.

I pushed open the door to her building and followed her inside. When we got to her room, someone had written on the small whiteboard outside her door. The single word said, *Murderer.*

I erased it with my hand, but not before she saw it. The color drained from her face, and she swayed on her feet. I ushered her inside, fury creating a red haze over my vision.

CHAPTER ELEVEN

WINTER

I closed my laptop, the last homework done for the day, when the door to my room opened. The scent of pizza wafted through the room, and I swiveled in my desk chair to grin at Piper as she entered, juggling several things. I jumped up and relieved her of the pizza box, and she tossed a bag and her backpack on her bed.

"I'm so glad you said you would be here tonight." Piper swiped a few blond strands of hair back that'd come loose from her ponytail. "I needed a girls' night in. Where's Shane? I was surprised when you said you were up for something tonight after he said he would be with you every night."

"He's working out with his brother. I told him I planned to do something with you in our room and not to worry."

A pensive look clouded her prefect features. "Hey, how are you doing? With everything."

She didn't need to elaborate. My life was crazy, and most students at Thane had either heard about the abduction or read the article about my mom in jail and how my sister's death was possibly my fault. "I'm fine, but I really don't want to talk about it. Can we just have a normal night?"

"I can do normal. Be prepared for the usual freshman questions, then."

I grinned, some of the heaviness leaving me. "Bring it. How's the boyfriend?"

Piper stayed with him most nights, which I understood, especially since she was a year older than me.

"John's good, but he went to play basketball with some of his friends, and I wasn't up for tagging along. We just finished a huge project for class, and I needed to blow off some steam." She grabbed the pizza and flipped the lid open, setting it on her desk. Then she pulled out paper plates from her stash and handed them to me. "Dig in."

She'd messaged me earlier, asking if I liked pepperoni pizza and if I was free. It was the perfect excuse for me to get Shane to do one of the workouts his brother had been hounding him about. Buried in homework at the time, I hadn't gotten dinner and had no plans to leave the room anyway.

"Thanks."

I loaded my plate, set it on my desk, then grabbed the Brita-filtered water we kept inside the fridge and passed it to her. She filled a cup, and we demolished a slice of pizza each before pausing for air.

"How are things going for you? Do you like your classes? I feel so bad that I haven't been around much. And I know we're not doing this, but you know you can message me if Shane isn't around. I don't always have to be with John."

"Thanks for saying that, but don't worry about it. I'm drowning in assignments anyway. It's keeping me busy. As for my classes, I like them well enough." I thought I would be happier in my art class, but it wasn't a big deal. The projects just weren't anything exciting. I wished that would change, as I'd had high hopes for Professor Elian.

"Okay, good. What about meeting people?" She took another bite, her blue eyes steady on me as she waited for my answer.

"I've met a few, and my brother is here, so it hasn't been too bad. I still miss home."

A bittersweet smile curved Piper's mouth, and she leaned back on her bed so her back rested against the wall. "I couldn't wait to get out. Things had escalated my senior year in high school between me and this guy I had a massive crush on. I thought he was my everything." She shook her head. "I couldn't have been more wrong."

"Really?" She'd piqued my interest. That was the stuff I'd missed by moving away. Not that I was complaining, because there was no way I would've wanted to stay there. Life had been so much better in LA with the Childress family. "What happened?"

She set her plate on her lap and grimaced. "I'm sure you've heard of Cole Savage from Shane. Cole's a big football star here. He and I were exclusive for a while during high school, and I read more into it than I should have. I knew he was going places, and I hitched my wagon to my best friend's plan to ride on the guys' coattails and become an NFL WAG."

"A what?"

"Wives and girlfriends of athletes." Piper waved the thought away. "It was Tracey's goal, and she's still on track to be that. Not with the other Savage brother, but with the new guy she's been dating, Dominick Reynolds. He's already in the MLB."

"But your boyfriend now isn't in sports, right?" I was just trying to follow her logic.

"No. He's athletic"—she laughed—"I do have a type, after all. After Cole crushed my soul, I realized I didn't want to be dependent on a man. I love my boyfriend, and he will be a highly sought-after architect—but so will I—before we get married."

I paused, my second slice of pizza halfway to my mouth. "When? Has he already proposed?"

She snorted. "He's talked about it—a lot. But I told him I

have no interest in marriage until I'm secure in my career. However, I agreed to move in with him next year."

"So living together but no legal commitments?"

"Yep. If I learned one thing from Cole, it's that I need to put my goals and desires before anyone else's or I'll never be happy."

"That's smart." I took a sip of water then put the cup back on my desk. "What the heck happened with Cole?" He was Shane's cousin. I didn't know him well, but it had to bother her that I was with someone who was part of Cole's inner circle and always would be.

"I don't know." She blew out a breath then tossed her empty plate onto her desk. "I was crazy about him. He was a god in our school—you know, those guys who are at the top. Everyone knew who he was and wanted to be with him. And when I was with him… it was this incredibly powerful feeling. That was something I didn't feel I had a lot of with my family shit going on. I never let on that things weren't great at home or that my dad was making one bad business decision after another. My mom was drinking wine nonstop."

"I'm sorry. I know firsthand how a crappy homelife can color everything around you." It had affected so many things for me—how I'd dealt with problems, pushed people away, and lashed out, unable to keep the pain, loneliness, and desperation I'd felt daily inside.

Sadness swam in her light eyes. "Yeah, I know. Summer shared some things with me back then. My parents were okay when I was young, and it was hard to understand why your mom was the way she was."

I rubbed at my chest, trying to alleviate the sudden ache her words caused. "Back to Cole—what happened with him that made you want to change?" I needed to steer the subject far away from my sister and what we'd been through.

"This other girl caught his eye. She was new, and nothing

bothered her. No matter how mean I was, or my friends, she just brushed it off. It was infuriating."

"What do you mean? You bullied her?" I had no room to judge, so I kept my features and voice as neutral as possible.

"Yep." She popped the P. "Me, Tracey, and some of our friends. I was so fucking devastated when Cole pushed me aside. He was cold, and his disdain when he talked to me cut me deep. I wanted to destroy her because she'd taken what I'd assumed was mine." She pushed out a breath. "God, I was a bitch."

"Well, you said it didn't bother her. So no harm, really, right?"

"They're still together and going strong, and they're this power couple anyway. I'm sure whatever I did back then was more of an annoying gnat rather than what I'd intended. Anyway, I keep my distance from him." The way her shoulders slumped revealed a deep sadness, as did the downward tilt to her mouth.

"Do you still love him?"

"No. I don't think so." Silence stretched between us for a minute. "Honestly, a part of me will always love him, but he's not the one for me. If I had ended up with him, he would've eclipsed me, and I would never have seen the future I'm laying out for myself. The sad truth is I don't think he ever loved me. Riley has his heart, and that's what cut me the most when I realized she wasn't a passing hookup."

"Does it bother you that Shane's been around?"

The sadness that'd been there a moment ago melted away with the easy laughter that spilled from her mouth. "No, not at all. I'm totally over being a part of that group. I changed over the summer, before coming to Thane, and I have to say it was for the better. I'm happy and know what I want to do with my life."

I relaxed. The last thing I wanted to do was make things hard for Piper. We weren't close, but I felt comfortable thinking of her as more than a roommate after our conversation. "I'm happy for you."

"Thanks." She closed the pizza box. "Want to watch a movie? I need to do something brainless after the past couple of days."

"Sure. I could use a break too." Even though I knew it would be temporary.

Too many unresolved things from the past were catching up with me. But that was part of why I came to Thane, to face my demons and lay them to rest. I just hoped I could do that without them taking me down.

Three days and nights had passed since my evening with Piper, and Shane was still staying with me. We'd grown closer, more comfortable with one another. And getting ready for bed and falling asleep in his arms had been so natural I couldn't imagine sleeping alone again.

My desire for him roared back to life as the fear faded, but I fought it. I didn't need that complication, or at least, not yet. Not only that, but I wasn't sure he felt the same. Things stood between us that I wasn't sure were fully resolved, and most of them—the way I used to treat him and his getting scrutinized by the police—were my fault.

Shane left early in the morning to work out with the team, or maybe it was only some of the football players. I hadn't paid close enough attention to what he'd said, just that he would return before dinner. I didn't have any plans, and I had some snacks and an apple in my room, which was all I would need until he returned.

It was Saturday, and I didn't want to stay on campus all

evening. When Shane knocked on the door and identified himself, I whipped it open and sucked in my breath. His broad shoulders spanned most of the threshold, a tight gray shirt stretching across them and highlighting his body in a way that made me dizzy. I shook myself free from the pull he seemed to have over me and stepped aside so he could enter.

"Hey, I know this is sort of odd, but I want to try to jog my memory about the day I lost my sister." I shared about the cabin at McMillan Lake, where my sister had died, and how that was where my kidnapper had taken me. "Will you take me there? My mom has a parole hearing soon, and I need to decide whether I'm going."

"If you think it'll help to go there, then let's do it."

I grabbed my keys and purse, and he threaded our fingers together as we left. It was something he'd been doing lately, and the way he held my hand was the most natural thing. I liked it. A lot.

It wasn't until we reached McMillan Lake that memories of my sister dying assaulted me. I remembered the hard shove, the air forced from my lungs from the impact. Then the splash. Not one but two. Flailing frantically, my fingernails digging into the wood piling beneath the dock. Then the timing skipped, and I was on the ground, pebbles digging into my skin as I reached for my sister. She stared sightlessly at me, the blue tinge to her mouth and nose alarming against the pallor of her skin. I heard fighting. A man and a woman, but I couldn't make out the words. All I could focus on was Summer and how much I needed her.

I was shivering by the time Shane pulled up along the curb and exited the SUV. He opened my door, swore when he saw my state, and pulled me into his arms. The warmth of his skin seeped into mine as he held me. We stood like that for I didn't know how long.

In time, I calmed, regaining control enough for him to release me but not all the way. He kept my hand in his, and I was grateful for the lifeline. The small connection made me feel protected and safe, as if he shared some of my burdens, lessening their weight.

The crime-scene tape had been removed. We walked to the cabin's front door, and Shane knocked. We waited a few minutes before he tried the doorknob, but it was locked. A light was on inside. Someone was clearly living there because I could make out a navy ball cap hanging off a chair.

When no one answered, I took Shane around back. "This is the door I left from and the room where I woke."

That door was also locked. He used a corner of his shirt to clear away some of the grime on the window, and we peered inside. It looked the same, a single bed the only furniture in sight. With not much to see, we left the cabin to explore the grounds instead.

"That's the dock you drew. Let's go out there. Maybe it'll help."

I nodded, anxiety a live wire under my skin. Then I shook my head. "I can't swim." *Shit.* That wasn't true. "I mean, I can. Just not here."

His brows climbed his forehead. "I won't let you fall in."

I shook my head furiously, backing away. "I can't."

"Okay." He shifted toward me, blocking the dock, and cupped my face. "It's okay. We don't have to go near the lake."

He held my gaze until I could regulate my breathing and push back some of the raw fear.

When I was better, he reclaimed my hand and turned us to walk parallel to the water but a reasonable distance from it so I could keep my panic at bay. I scanned the sparse grass interspersed with bare dirt patches.

"An old canoe used to sit over there. It's gone." I pointed to a spot by a fallen log, and a hazy and fleeting memory of my sister and me hiding behind it came forward then disappeared.

A willow tree leaned over the water. It was bigger, but I could still see Summer hanging from the low branch, running back and forth like she was swinging on it. I drowned in the memory, missing my sister and not wanting to come up for air until Shane's strong arms wrapped around my waist. The heat of his body eased the tension, and I took a full breath, probably my first since we'd arrived.

"Nothing I remember helps with my decision about the parole hearing."

"Are you ready to go, then?"

"Yes." I wanted to leave. My sister wouldn't want me to stay. We'd hated the place. I felt it deep in my bones.

We drove to a small café, and after placing our orders, we sat at one of the outside tables with a big red shade umbrella over-head. It didn't take long for our food to come out, and I nibbled on a fry, contemplating what I wanted to ask Shane. He and I had gone to school together, for a little while, anyway. His family probably knew mine.

"Does your mom know about me?"

He swallowed then looked at me, his deep-blue eyes branding my soul, seeing too much in the way they always did.

I didn't think he was following. "About my mom, that she's in prison. Did your mom know her?"

He set down his half-finished burger. "Yeah, she did. Mom said Katrina struggled after your dad died and that's when they lost touch."

His words were gentle, and he said nothing about the drugs or the men who had come in and out of our apartment we moved into after Dad died. But he knew. I could tell in the pity that flashed across his face before he could hide it. I hated that, but I didn't have the energy to confront him about it.

When his phone rang, he glanced at it and shoved it in his pocket, a frown marring his face.

"You can answer the call. I don't mind."

"I don't want to. It's Joe."

"What does he want? Is he still pressuring you about going into business together?"

"He wants me to sell my Range Rover and use the money to invest in the business."

That was weird. "I thought you had money. Why would you need to sell your car?"

"My grandad has money. My uncle too. I don't. And if my family finds out I've given even a dime to Joe, they'll lose their minds."

"I bet your family isn't thrilled about you talking to me either." A wave of guilt hit me. I couldn't imagine his family being happy about us spending time together. Maybe I wasn't the father who abandoned him, but I wasn't a good part of his childhood. At the very least, I could let him know I regretted who I'd been to him before. "I'm so sorry, Shane, for everything I did to you when we were kids. I was horrible, and I wish I could take it back."

He picked his food back up. "It's okay. I'm fine. I survived, obviously." He shrugged, and a small, sad smile tilted one corner of his mouth.

A memory flashed through my mind of a day when I had told him I wanted to apologize for some awful thing I'd done and give him a kiss, then I had left him blindfolded and puckered up. The memory hit me with brutal clarity, and shame filled me. "You survived?" There were so many things I'd done to him that I wished I could take back. I was a different person than I had been then. My heart ached.

His expression became shuttered in that guarded way he had of locking me out of what he was feeling. I hated it because it scared me. I'd tormented him—the kid I'd always felt could see inside me—wanting to hurt him so he would feel what I had.

I shoved my food away, unable to eat another bite because I knew what he wasn't telling me. I'd pushed him too close to the edge, and he'd dipped a toe into the abyss of despair I'd lived in. Cold seeped in, the kind that got under my skin and infected the very marrow of my bones. "I'm so sorry. For everything. Please forgive me, Shane."

CHAPTER TWELVE

SHANE

The image of that damn blue baseball hat hanging off the chair in the cottage's front room flashed in my mind. I'd finished my food, and Winter pushed hers around in the basket, pretending to eat. The apology she'd given me was a salve over jagged wounds that hadn't fully healed. But most of all, her traumatized look when she'd realized how her bullying had affected me helped—a lot. And I needed to let it go, to forgive her. I didn't hold on to grudges as tightly as my brother and cousins did. Or I tried not to.

"Are you finished?" I asked.

She nodded, and I took our garbage and tossed it in the trash.

"I need to go back to the football house for a minute. Do you want to come with me?"

"Sure." She stood and fell into step beside me as we headed to my SUV.

The drive back went quickly, as we were both lost in our thoughts. When we arrived, I ushered her to my room then went to make a call to Joe, one I needed to be alone for. I went down to the kitchen and hit Redial. He answered on the second ring.

"Are you staying at a cabin at McMillan Lake?"

"Hey, Shane. Thanks for calling me back, and yeah, I am. Why? Do you need a place to take girls back to?"

His response hit me wrong, but I couldn't figure out why. I ignored it and went on to my next question. "Do you know about a drowning that happened when I was a kid? I think it was a girl around my age."

"No. I would've been in Chicago then. This is my first time returning to California since leaving your mom. And that was before you were even born."

I rested a hip against the counter, unsure of what else to say to him. *Do I want to tell him about being brought into the station again?*

"Did you get the money?"

"Not yet." The words were bitter, and I grimaced as our conversation turned.

"The house isn't going to stay on the market forever. We need to get our bid in."

Something didn't feel right about that. Why was this house so important? There had to be others, and while I understood why he wanted to get the business running as soon as possible, the way he was going about it bothered me. I made an excuse, got off the phone, then took the stairs two at a time to return to my room. I didn't want to sell my car, and with all Joe's pressure, I felt backed into a corner.

I had the loan paperwork. Not that it would do me any good, but I was running out of options.

When I returned to my room, Winter lay on her side on my bed. The sight of her did something to me. I liked seeing her in my bed, more so than I would've thought. I paused by the door and studied how her strawberry-blond hair spilled across my pillow and her long, toned legs bent slightly at the knees. I fought the urge to go to her and run my hand along her smooth, silky skin. I wanted to feel her tremble with desire from my touch.

But that wasn't why she was there. I shoved down my intense need for her and smiled when she opened her eyes and found me standing there.

"Hey," she said.

Her soft and raspy voice drew me close with how much I wanted to touch her. "Hey yourself. Tired?"

She twisted so she was partially on her back, scooting over so I had room. "Yeah, I didn't sleep much last night, and today wore me out."

Emotionally, probably more than anything. "You can stay here tonight if you want."

"I would like that. Thanks." She sat up and slipped off her shoes.

They fell with a thud on the floor as a knock sounded at my door. When I opened it, Brad was on the other side, one of the defensive ends who shared a room with Tucker down the hall.

"What's up?" I blocked Winter from sight and went into the hall to hear what he had to say. He had better be quick. I wanted to get back to her.

"Professor Elian came around looking for you, but no one knew where you were. She got pissed off and left."

"Okay, thanks." My sleeping with her was a loose secret and not important. Her showing up wasn't great, though.

"And some guy who said his name was Joe."

"Thanks, man."

He grunted in response then went back to his room, and I returned to mine, locking the door behind me. I didn't need my brother, or anyone else, barging in without notice. When I turned around, it was to find Winter curled on her side again, fast asleep, and all I wanted to do was slide in next to her.

I removed my shoes and exchanged jeans for shorts, discarding my shirt before joining her. My bed was bigger than the one in her room, allowing us to sleep on it without touching. I pulled back the covers and got in next to her, trying not to wake her.

I wasn't careful enough, because her eyelids slowly lifted, then her hand slid over to rest on my chest. I didn't dare move, not sure what she wanted. But when her hand inched lower, I lightly encircled her wrist, holding her hooded gaze. "You agreed things were strictly business between us."

She shrugged one shoulder. "They were, but I don't care. I just want you."

My mind warred over the right thing to do until she climbed on top of me and pulled her shirt over her head. She won.

Her eyes darkened as my hands trailed over her ribs to cup her perfect breasts and roll her nipples. A sexy moan escaped her, and my body strained for more.

"God, you're gorgeous."

I explored the softness of her skin as she moved her hips, increasing the friction. The heat of her drove me crazy. I sat up, wanting her impossibly closer. My hand gripped the back of her neck, and I took her mouth in a hungry kiss. Her lips parted, and the first touch of her tongue fueled me to take more.

I wanted all her clothes off. With an arm around her waist, I lifted her, missing the heat and friction instantly. A hard tug, and I had her shorts over her hips. She helped, and we wrestled them and her panties off until she was naked and sitting on me again. Her hips moved automatically, and I groaned from how good she felt.

Her fingernails dug into my shoulders as she rode me, her heat tempting me to tear my shorts off and plunge into her, but not yet. I wanted to watch her fall apart first. I kissed down her neck, the sharp nip of my teeth making her cry out in pleasure.

I wanted to touch her everywhere and slipped my hand

between us, parting her slick folds to swirl a gentle caress over her sensitive bundle of nerves. She was warm and wet and so incredible. I teased her, making her head fall back, hair cascading in a thick curtain I wanted to wrap around my fist.

Her lower back arched as I sank a finger into her tight heat, her breaths coming in little puffs. I eased in another then pumped them in a slow caress, making her gasp. I urged her closer, curling my fingers deep inside, consumed by how much I wanted her.

She bucked against me, clinging to my shoulders. The sight of her riding my hand was incredible and fucking erotic. I couldn't take it anymore. She whimpered when I withdrew my fingers, but I needed to be inside her like I needed my next breath. I leaned over and grabbed a condom from the top drawer of my dresser. Then I lifted her and wrestled with my shorts as her hands tugged with me. Laughter spilled from her lips, and I paused, wanting to capture her image in my memory.

When I had the condom on, she lifted to her knees, and I positioned myself at her entrance. She sank slowly down. When our gazes caught and held, our connection snapped into place like a live wire. She sucked in a breath, and I could only guess she felt as branded by me as I did by her.

Hands on her hips, I guided her but let her set the rhythm. Her hands splayed on my chest, and the sight of her compelled me to flip her onto her back, but I held out for as long as I could. I increased the tempo between us, passion building to nearly impossible heights. Her breathy little moans and her body clenching mine had me slipping my hand between us to swirl a gentle caress over her sensitive nub. I took her mouth in a drugging kiss, swallowing her scream as she squeezed my body like a vise.

Goddamn. I flipped her onto her back and increased the tempo, my hips slamming against her. I broke the kiss, moaning against her skin as I chased her climax with the most powerful release I'd ever had.

I collapsed on top of her then rolled onto my side, taking her body with me. A shocking thought hit me and rearranged my entire world—*I'm never letting her go.*

87

CHAPTER THIRTEEN

WINTER

I woke shivering, missing the heat from Shane's body, and turned to find him hunched over his desk, filling out a form online. The sun was barely up, and weak rays filtered through the window, helping him see. I watched him, neck bent, fingers moving over the keys swiftly, before I scooted back and yanked the blanket hard. My back was against the wall, and Shane stopped what he was doing to look at me. His hair was messed in the sexiest of ways, either from sleep or my hands.

"Hey, sorry I woke you."

I shook my head, a small smile curving my mouth. "I don't mind."

I took in everything about him, from the tattoo on his chest over his right pec to the ones that covered his shoulder and trailed down one arm. Everything about him was gorgeous, and my body heated with banked desire. But I didn't think that was the time, not with the lines between his eyebrows and those bracketing his mouth. He raked his hands through his hair. Whatever he was working on seemed to cause him stress.

"What are you doing?"

"I'm trying to fill out a small business loan application."

"Why?" The dots weren't connecting.

"It's for that business Joe—my bio dad—wants to start with me. Phoenix, too, but that's not happening. It's either secure this loan or sell my Range Rover, which I don't want to do."

"Are you sure you want to be involved in this? You seem conflicted." I drew my knees to my chest and looped my arms around them.

"I want to try to have a relationship with Joe. It's something I've always wanted, even if Phoenix doesn't."

The wish for a father connected us in ways I'd never imagined. "I understand. I wonder more often than I like what my life would have been like if mine hadn't died." I hesitated then decided to go for it. "But if Joe is asking too much of you, is it worth it? You should be able to have a relationship with him without the pressure of starting a business and figuring out how to fund it."

"Trust me, that's what I'm wrestling with. He's just so adamant that this is what he wants to do, create a legacy for me and Phoenix. I think it's because he isn't playing football and is desperate for something to do with his life."

"Maybe." I thought back to how it had been with my foster family in the beginning. They had shown me unconditional love repeatedly without asking for anything in return other than for me to try to be happy. I didn't like what he was describing with his bio dad. "But a relationship with you shouldn't come at a cost."

He closed his laptop and stood, muscles bunching and rippling in a mouthwatering display. Tight black boxer briefs molded to him, leaving little to the imagination. His eyes dilated, telling me what he wanted, and I couldn't be more on board. I tossed the covers aside for him to come back to bed. A low sound of approval rumbled from his throat as his gaze visually caressed me. Other than the panties I'd pulled on, I was naked.

He climbed into bed facing me and looked his fill. My body responded without him touching me, softening, an ache pulsing in my core. I shivered when he trailed the back of his hand over the curve of my thigh. One touch from him, and my desire ignited. He watched me, his dark-blue eyes nearly eclipsed by his pupils, raw hunger burning within.

I mimicked the path he trailed along my body, enjoying the firmness of his bicep, his abs, his thigh, and every dip and valley of muscle as I explored him. Then he cupped the back of my neck and pulled me to him so my nipples rubbed against his chest. He lowered his mouth to mine slowly, flaming the fire between us to an inferno. I buried my hands in his thick, dark hair, gently tugging the strands.

He applied a slight pressure with his fingers at my nape, tilting my head for a better angle to deepen the kiss. I moaned, and he swallowed the sound. Then I felt him hook a finger under the waistband of my panties before he tugged them off, never breaking our kiss.

I slid my leg over his. It wasn't enough, and he grasped the back of my thigh, pulling it higher. His hand caressed my skin, teasing touches just out of reach of the apex of my thighs. He had me squirming against him. I couldn't get close enough, and a whimper escaped me.

I pressed my breasts against his hard chest and kissed him like it was my last breath. Every nerve ending was on fire as he explored me, leaving no part of me untouched. He set the pace, a slow rhythm that had me aching and my heart swelling, anticipating every touch. My core throbbed. I wanted him inside me. I begged, pleaded, and he brought me to the brink of orgasm more than once before I felt his hard length pressing against my entrance.

I moaned, arching into him as he pushed inside me. Sensations built, and I met his insatiable need with a raging thirst of my own. The room spun as he thrust deep. I tightened around him, and my body exploded as I screamed his name. It didn't take him long to chase my orgasm with his own.

His large, heavy body collapsed on top of mine, and I welcomed his weight for as long as possible. I trailed my fingers over his powerful back, tracing soothing circles along the dips and bulges of muscles until he shifted to his side, taking me with him. We lay together for a while before we got up to dispose of the condom and clean up.

Back in bed, Shane wrapped me in his embrace. My eyes slowly closed, and I was utterly content.

I drifted in and out of sleep, my head resting on Shane's arm. My finger lightly traced the stubble on his jaw. He slept, even with my gentle touch. Dark hair fell across his forehead, and I brushed it back. He really was beautiful. Everything about him was chiseled, strong, and memorable. As I stared at Shane's face, the image of him as a boy superimposed over it, and I let the memory sweep me away.

My stomach growled, and I recalled the constant sharp pang of hunger when I was younger. Particularly, one time when Mom had stuffed a sack lunch into Summer's backpack, giving her the last piece of bread. She hadn't seen Mom do it, or she would have shared. I hadn't wanted to tell her because I didn't want my sister to be as hungry as I was.

My memory skipped to when Mom hadn't been home for two days and we'd had no food in the house. Summer and I were used to getting ourselves out of the house and on the bus without her there. Mrs. C. didn't know we were alone, or she would have fed us. Maybe she was away visiting her family. We were confused about what we should do.

Shane had sat nearby, and I remembered being so angry because his mom had always packed his lunches. Sometimes, she even wrote him notes. I knocked his food on the ground and called him names. I got sent to the principal's office. But that wasn't a bad thing. Whenever I'd told her why I'd done what I'd done, that I'd just been so hungry, she would open her drawer and share her snacks with me.

I sat up, scooting away from Shane on the bed, self-loathing in full effect.

I hadn't meant to be mean to him, not really. I'd been so hungry, hurt, and lost that I'd taken it out on the kid who'd struggled to speak without stuttering. I'd targeted his weakness because he had family who loved him and I'd wanted to drag him down to my level. Even then, I'd craved something from him. I just hadn't understood it or gone about anything in the right way.

Fat tears rolled down my face, and my body shook with ugly sobs. I hated what Mom had done to us. We'd endured so many things until she'd snuffed out my sister's life and ended her reign of torture and hatred.

"Hey, what's wrong?" he asked, evidently having woken up.

Shane's arm went around me as he sat up, and he pulled me close. I rested my face against his chest and wrestled for control over my emotions, taking the Kleenex box he offered. I mopped up my face and released a stuttering breath after a few more sniffles.

"I just remembered one of the times I was horrible to you. I was so hungry, and you had food. I was jealous and miserable and took it out on you."

"Stop torturing yourself." His deep voice rumbled through his chest, and he cupped my head, holding me to him. "It's in the past. Over and done with. You have no reason to keep revisiting it."

We stayed like that, with me clinging to him, wrapped in the strength of his embrace, for a long time. Sunlight streamed through the large window. It wasn't until his phone vibrated on his dresser that I untangled myself so he could answer it.

While he talked to his brother—I could hear some of the conversation—I busied myself with gathering the wadded-up tissues before getting up and throwing them away. He hung up as I looked for where we'd flung the rest of my clothes.

"I have to go to a family dinner tonight."

His expression was guarded, and I knew it was because of me. "Please don't do that. I have a family that loves me now. I just didn't then, other than my sister. I'm okay, I promise."

The wall fell away, and he smiled then motioned for me to climb back into bed with him. I did. *Who could pass up the chance to touch perfection?* He could make me forget my name when I looked at him.

"I don't want to leave you alone when I head home." His fingers combed through my hair, snagging a few times on the knots from sleeping and all the amazing sex.

"I'll be fine."

"I can ask Damon and Sky to hang out with you."

"No. Please don't. It'll only be a few hours. I can call my brother and hang out with him. It'll be fine. Promise."

He waited for a beat then gave in. "How do you want to spend our Sunday?"

CHAPTER FOURTEEN

SHANE

I spent the day with Winter, teaching her more self-defense moves, then we lay on my bed and watched movies on my laptop. If someone had told me when I was younger that I would end up with Winter Patten in my room, have sex with her, and watch movies, I would've said no fucking way. But there she was, and there we were.

It was time to take Winter back to her dorm so I could leave for dinner with Phoenix, Aspen, and Mom at Grandad's. With our fingers threaded together, we walked at a slow pace. I didn't want to leave her, but bringing her with me wasn't an option. Not with how Mom felt about her, which was justified—until I had a chance to explain some things and she gave Winter a chance. But I would not take her to Grandad's. That would be like throwing her to the wolves.

As we turned the corner and crossed the quad, a feeling of being watched itched across my skin. I glanced over my shoulder and narrowed my eyes when I spotted Cindy about ten feet behind us. She needed to take a hint, and I would clarify how done with her I was.

I released Winter's hand and wrapped my arm around her

waist, pulling her against my side. She leaned into me, a perfect fit. Cindy kept pace, slowing when we reached the door to Winter's building. Before I held it open, I turned her in my arms and took her mouth in a steamy kiss. We were both breathless by the time I reluctantly broke it.

"What was that for?" she murmured, her voice raspy with desire.

I ran the pad of my thumb over her full lower lip, wanting to go in for more rather than leave her for a few hours. "Because I wanted to." I couldn't give her the whole reason. I did want to kiss her. That urge was always there, but I wanted to put on a show for Cindy. The woman needed to back off and realize we would never happen again.

My fingers curled around the handle of the door, and I pulled it open. With a hand on the small of her back, I followed Winter inside and ensured she got safely to her room.

"Lock this behind you, and don't open it for anyone unless you know who it is."

"Okay, Dad." Winter rolled her eyes then laughed. "Have a good dinner with your family. And please, don't call your friends about me. I'll chat with Jaxon and get dinner with him or something."

"Have him come to your room and pick you up."

"Oh, trust me. He'll be all over that. He was upset that I didn't call him immediately after everything happened."

That didn't sound right. "Why didn't you?"

Her cheeks turned a pretty shade of pink. "I wasn't thinking straight. Also, Jaxon was away for a few days meeting Max's parents, and I didn't want to call him all hysterical so he would rush to my side." She waved her hands between us. "And when I saw you at the police station, my thoughts got even more muddled."

"That was a shitshow."

She shrugged. "Yeah, but you always make me forget everything else when I'm around you."

I grinned because what guy wouldn't want to hear that from a beautiful woman like Winter? I pressed a kiss to her lips. "Lock up. I'll check in when I'm on my way back."

"Thanks, and have fun." She gave me a little wave then shut the door. I heard the lock engage before I jogged down the stairs to the first floor. Once outside, I didn't have to look hard for Cindy. She waited on the steps, seething.

I took her arm tightly and pulled her off the steps, moving her a few feet from the path before spinning her to face me. Then I released her. "Why are you following me when I specifically told you we're done?" I knew she could hear the fury behind my words.

"The girl you're seeing isn't good for you. She murdered her sister." She flung out her hand, her eyes huge and a little unfocused. "Didn't you see the blog post?"

"I don't care about any bullshit on the internet. This"—I motioned between us—"needs to stop. If you don't leave me alone, I'll go to the dean."

Laughter spilled from her lips, and I fought the urge to take a step back from her crazy.

"I know your family." Her voice lowered, and her pupils seemed to grow larger. "If you think I won't tell your mom about our affair, about everything, you're wrong."

"It doesn't matter. That's not the threat you think it is. I don't care what you tell her. My mom will be furious and disgusted with you, not me. The one who stands to lose the most, meaning your job, is you." I'd said what I needed to and moved around her and back onto the path. *Screw that.* I needed to stop engaging with her. It didn't do any good. It would be better to follow through with my threat.

I hadn't gone more than three feet before she called after me.

"Fine. Be with a murderer. You're exactly alike since you're one too."

I stuttered a step before catching myself. *Fuck.* I tried not to think too deeply. If I did, the fact that I'd killed someone, by accident or not, would replay with savage clarity, looping through my thoughts. I fought to put one foot in front of the other so she wouldn't see me bend in half from the pain. I didn't have time for a mental breakdown, not when I had to go to a family dinner and pretend everything was okay.

The drive home helped me get my head on straight and shove the pain and despair away from what had happened when I'd hit Luke. I got to Grandad's after everyone else had arrived, as I was ten minutes late, thanks to my argument with Cindy.

I parked and jogged up the steps that led to the grand front door, a combination of wrought iron, glass, and wood. It was a statement piece and very fitting for the entrance to Grandad's mansion.

The porch and chairs out front had been for our nona and something Grandad had taken meticulous care of himself. The staff didn't touch her chair. That was all Grandad. Little things like that showed us how deeply he cared, and we needed those reminders when he was his usual gruff and dictatorial self.

Without ringing the bell, I walked inside. It was easy to find where everyone was by following the voices. Aspen's laughter rang out like a balm to my soul. Things said in the past between Grandad and both Aspen and Phoenix could have torn our family apart. They hadn't. Aspen hadn't let them.

I entered the family room to find everyone except Grandad congregating on the couches around the coffee table. Leaving behind the worries plaguing me, I grinned, hiding my mountain of problems as heads turned my way.

"Hi, Shane." Mom stood and wrapped me in a tight hug. Her hand lingered on my cheek before she stepped back, releasing me.

"Hey, Mom."

She gave the best hugs, and it was enough to beat the darkness back so I could mask it effectively. I turned to Phoenix, slapped him on the shoulder, then hugged Aspen.

"Where's Grandad?"

"He's still in his office," Mom said.

"I'm starving. I'll go get him." It was the opportunity I'd been looking for to get him alone. There were things that needed to be discussed. I couldn't shake the sly comments from Joe that we had mob ties who could fix things for me if needed.

"Hey"—Phoenix separated from everyone and intercepted me from going to the office—"we need to talk."

We made an excuse and went into the living room where no one could hear us.

"It's time we confront Grandad."

My gaze swung to my brother's. "Okay." I knew what I wanted to talk to him about but doubted it was the same thing Phoenix had on his mind. "Want to give me a little more information?"

"About keeping his nose out of relationships that don't concern him."

"I thought you'd already had a conversation with him and had forgiven him."

"I'm still pissed. It wasn't enough, and I need to rehash things. The only reason I'm talking to him is because of Aspen."

"She is your better half," I teased, eliciting a smile from my brother. It helped, but I could still feel the anger rolling off him. I got it.

"We're on the same page?"

"Yeah." I agreed—more needed to be said.

"Let's get this over with." Phoenix maneuvered past me.

I glanced back.

Mom's head was close to Aspen's, and when she looked up,

her wide smile slowly melted away as she caught sight of my face. "Is everything okay?"

"Yeah." I tried to reassure her, but one look at my brother, and she understood.

Phoenix clenched and unclenched his fists. I bumped him aside with my shoulder and moved toward the hallway that led to Grandad's office, not bothering to check if my brother followed.

The door was open, and I entered first, Phoenix behind me. Grandad sat at his desk, his white button-down's sleeves rolled and pushed past his elbows as his fingers flew over the keyboard. Even when he worked from home, his salt-and-pepper hair and clothes were immaculate. Authority and power radiated from him. The large mahogany desk stood sentry between Grandad and us.

"Grandad." It was the only warning I gave as Phoenix and I barged in. My tone was enough, though ambushing him completely wouldn't benefit anyone.

"Boys." His fingers pounded the keys until the swoosh sounded, signaling an email had been sent. Only then did he raise his gaze to meet ours. "Have a seat." He shut his laptop with a quiet click then steepled his hands.

Phoenix hesitated, and I fought to not roll my eyes while I sat across from Grandad. We waited until my brother finished wrestling with his emotions enough to take the seat next to me.

"You boys seem to have something to say…" Grandad left the statement hanging.

I glanced at Phoenix, noting how the muscle along his jaw jumped. It might be better to circle around to his grievances in a moment so he could calm down—hopefully.

I cleared my throat. "You do a lot for this family, and we appreciate it. But we need to clear the air about how you overstep and try to control things when it's not your place to do so."

Grandad lifted one eyebrow in challenge, his formidable personality front and center.

But we were there for a reason, so I pushed forward. "We need to establish ground rules for involvement."

"Think carefully about what you have to say," he growled.

"You don't have the upper hand here, old man." Phoenix matched his tone. "You tried to destroy my relationship and influence whether I became a dad."

Fuck. The conversation was going nowhere fast. Sometimes I resented the peacemaker role I'd been forced into with my family. "That's a prime example of overstepping." I held up my hand and hurried my words as Grandad opened his mouth. "Please just hear us out. If we're going to be a better family moving forward, and we need to be with the baby coming, then we have to come to a clear understanding of what's expected—from all of us."

We should've brought Mom in, too, but she was enjoying her time with Aspen. I hadn't missed the dark circles under her eyes. I would have to fill her in later. She would hound us both if we didn't.

"I don't know everything that happened with your relationship with your daughter Linda, our cousins' mom, but look what it cost you? Aunt Linda, for one." I needed to help Phoenix out, and I would do my best to paint the pattern Grandad seemed stuck in, highlighting all he'd lost. "And you have no involvement with Cole and Damon and probably never will."

"Those were extenuating circumstances. Lucas, while a good man, was not the one for Linda. He did not love her in the way she needed."

I knew that was all he would be willing to divulge. We'd heard some of the problems. His daughter, our aunt Linda, had had serious issues with drugs and depression. If there had been more, I wasn't aware of them, but Phoenix and I had held front-row seats to what had happened in our cousins' family life growing up. I couldn't lay all the blame at Grandad's feet, not with his daughter. But it was a stepping stone to what he continued to do with the rest of his family, and it was where I intended to start.

"And with Mom? You got involved in her relationship with Joe. You denied us the right to have a father who might have wanted to be there for us." That was a long shot, but I was using it as an example anyway.

Grandad's lip lifted in a sneer, and I felt rather than saw Phoenix aligning with him on the topic. It would be a touch-and-go one, not something that would serve our purpose.

"That isn't what we need to focus on," Phoenix interjected.

It was—it showed a pattern. But I backed off because we needed to circle back to his grievances, and he had calmed down enough to take over the conversation.

"You have no right to involve yourself in any matters regarding Aspen or my child. If you have concerns, they need to come to me. They are my family, and if you want to be a part of it, to be there as my daughter grows, you need to respect the boundaries in place. Because what you said to Aspen about terminating the pregnancy, and ending our relationship, made me want to never speak with you again. I'm still on the fence, and the only reason I'm here is because Aspen forgave you and wants me to try. I'm still not sure it's worth it."

"I will admit that I overstepped."

Phoenix snorted, and I fought against rolling my eyes.

"That's the understatement of the year," my brother said.

I shot him a reproachful look. He wasn't wrong, but comments like that didn't help. "You have to trust us to make the right decisions and, if we make a mistake, be there to support us—if we ask for help."

Grandad's eyes hardened, and the fire inside them fizzled. "What you're saying is you only need me for financial aid."

If I ever could have forgotten, that was a strong reminder

that stubbornness ran in our family. "No. That wasn't what I meant." He did have a point, though, and I sighed. "You are always there for us when we need you most—case in point, my legal problems this year. I needed your support, and you gave it willingly. It's not just about money. I might not have had the funds to hire your lawyer, but Uncle Lucas wouldn't have charged me for anything I needed."

"You know I will always be there for you." His voice was suspiciously gruff, and I knew that the last part about Uncle Lucas's willingness to step in had hit home.

"Yes. But things have to change." I kicked at my brother's foot. "For all of us. You have to stop trying to control the relationships we have, even if you have a strong conviction that something could go drastically wrong. Rather than acting to solve a potential issue, talk to us, hear what we say, and respect our decisions. And we'll do the same."

He grunted, and I took it for the agreement I knew he meant.

"I'm not over what you tried to do," Phoenix said through clenched teeth.

Grandad kept silent, observing my brother and looking for weaknesses he could exploit. When he found none, he offered a single nod. "You're right. I apologize for attempting to buy Aspen's cooperation and influence the outcome of her pregnancy."

Phoenix mimicked the nod. "And going forward?"

"You're both young men capable of making your own decisions."

And mistakes. I almost laughed because I saw Grandad bite down at the end of his sentence. I knew he'd been about to say more but had thought better of it. *Progress.* I would take it.

"Now that we've cleared that up…" A stab of guilt hit me. I hadn't gone into detail with Grandad about my involvement with Joe. I would, but something still held me back, and I listened to that instinct. We'd made progress. I didn't want to go backward by making him blow up about my biological father.

It wasn't the best recourse, but I would stick to it temporarily. I did intend to talk to him about it, just not immediately. However, I did want to know more about something Joe had mentioned.

"Are we connected to the Bennett crime family? The mafia?"

Full disclosure was something we all needed to work on. Both Grandad and I were taking tentative steps forward. While he'd held back the dangerous tidbit—assuming it was true—I still had things to share about Joe. None of us were perfect.

Phoenix's head swiveled in my direction. I hadn't shared with him what Joe had told me, and rather than believe our dad, I wanted Grandad to tell us if it was true or not.

"I won't ask how you found out about that." Grandad's stare was cold, and we both knew he suspected who had told me. He was right. It was best to leave that topic alone for the time being. "Yes, my third cousin is head of the Bennett crime family."

"Why is this the first time I'm hearing of this?" Wariness coated Phoenix's question.

"Sal Bennett is a monster. There was no reason to make you or my daughters aware of him—especially Linda." He closed his eyes briefly. "Sal's wife is dead. How do you think that happened? I've heard the rumors, and let me tell you, I believe them. When he deemed Maria Bennett as no longer useful, he killed her."

"They have people on the police—"

Grandad's fist slammed onto the desk, making his pen jump from the surface. "Never get involved with Sal. He will only bring you down. If you're asked, we have no relation to that family. Did a cop approach you, or the feds?"

"No." I held his gaze, letting him see the truth in that one word. "It's just something I heard."

His hand flattened on the desk and remained there. "I have nothing to do with Sal and never have. My business is free of mob involvement, and I want to keep it that way. If Sal found an advantage to using our family ties for the business, I would sell it in a heartbeat. I'm begging you to leave that thread alone. Don't pull on it, because it'll only lead to death and destruction."

"I won't. I just wanted to know if it was true. That's the only reason I asked." *Why does Joe know about that part of our family? Was he involved with them, or does he owe them money? Is that the reason for his urgency to "start the business"?*

"Sal has kids close to your age. I don't think they're as bad as him, but they're still mafia. And as long as Sal is head of the Bennett family, they're a problem too." He closed his eyes briefly before bouncing them between Phoenix and me. "No matter what happens, never go to them. Always come to me."

"We will." Phoenix's gaze bored into the side of my head, his promise to Grandad weighing in the air between us.

"I know you haven't shut things down with Joe, Shane." Grandad dropped his own bomb. "I need you to be careful where he's concerned. I wanted him out of your mother's life, and yours, for more than one reason."

The hair on the back of my neck rose at the ominous tone in Grandad's voice. But I was already six feet under and lying next to Luke with the number of situations I'd found myself in that year. I hardly thought the handful of meetings I'd had with Joe would cause more damage.

"Are you in some sort of trouble?" The harshness I expected from him never came, only worry that added lines to his aging face.

"No. I'm fine. Things are… fine." I couldn't tell Grandad about Joe wanting money. Even worse, I knew I shouldn't be associating with my bio dad after everything that had happened, but a part of me wanted to know him, to give him a second chance and see how it played out.

That wasn't the only reason I had to keep Joe's frequent meetings and demands a secret. After everything Grandad had pulled with Aspen and Phoenix, I didn't want to create more problems with my family. I just wanted them to get along. And if I gave the slightest hint that Joe wanted to start a business with me, I knew the chaos it would bring to my family.

CHAPTER SIXTEEN

WINTER

I threw my arms up as my ball knocked over all the pins for a strike. The place was packed with college students, but it wasn't so loud that I didn't hear Jaxon grunt behind me. I laughed, whirling around, and smirked at my brother. "Never underestimate me."

Jaxon gained his feet, stretching to his six-foot-one height. "Big words from someone who had three gutter balls."

"Please." I snorted then grinned at Max. "I was just warming up. There's no stopping all this awesomeness."

Max laughed, and Jaxon glared over his shoulder as he retrieved his ball from the return.

"Don't encourage her." Jaxon winked at me before stepping up to the line.

Falling into a seat next to Max, I said, "I'm glad we finally met. Jaxon has told me about you, and I've wanted to do this for a while."

"It's overdue." Max rested his arm on the back of my chair. "He's really happy you're here. And that you called to get together. We're both pretty happy about that."

Max was impossible not to like. He was someone who drew

people to him with his charm and charisma. "We should make bowling and crappy pizza dinners a weekly tradition."

"What's this?" Jaxon strolled over, hands in his pockets.

I didn't need to look at his score to know he'd picked up a strike. I never beat him. He was a natural at bowling but didn't take himself seriously and kept it fun.

"We're making Sunday bowling and dinner a weekly event," Max filled him in then turned back to me. "Will you be bringing your boyfriend with you?"

My gaze darted to Jaxon, gauging his reaction. *He hasn't told him it was Shane? Or has he?* There was no judgment, and I relaxed. "Maybe eventually. But for now, I would rather it be the three of us because I'm selfish like that." I grinned, bumping my shoulder into Max's side.

I did want to get to know Max more without Shane there. But I also craved time with Jaxon. We needed to make our drawing in the quad a weekly event too. I would talk to him about that later.

Max got up to bowl, and Jaxon took his place beside me. "Well?"

I laughed. "Seriously, you know I like him. And he treats you right, which I needed to see for myself." He also watched Jaxon when my brother didn't know. They fit. "I'm happy for you because it seems like you found a good guy."

"And he's hot."

I smacked his stomach, only making his teasing grin grow. We stayed another hour before they walked me back to my room. My cheeks hurt from how much I'd laughed. Hanging out with them was just what I needed.

It wasn't five minutes after they left that someone knocked on my door. *Perfect timing.* I knew it would be Shane, as it was hours after he'd left for dinner with his family. I yanked open the door, expecting to find him standing there, filling the doorway with a powerful punch of lust, only to experience the uncomfortable letdown of seeing Professor Elian.

"Ah, hi, Professor Elian." *What is she doing here, and how does she know where my room is? Or maybe she doesn't?* "Are you looking for someone else on this floor?" *Please be mistaken and want to talk to another person in a different room.*

She stepped closer, inches from my face and across the threshold so I couldn't shut the door. The strong scent of alcohol wafted off her. Her eyes were bloodshot, and her hair was disheveled.

"Are you okay?"

"No," she slurred and stumbled past me, her bag clipping me in the hip as she invited herself in.

The door slipped from my fingers as I turned toward her. She glanced around the room, her body swaying before she locked onto me, and I gasped at the hatred pulling her lips into a sneer. She flung an oversized shoulder bag onto my bed, but my focus snapped back to her with her next words.

"I'm sleeping with Shane. Me." She pointed at me, taking an unsteady step forward, then pressed her thumb to unlock her screen and held up her phone.

The picture she brandished burned into my retinas. It showed Professor Elian lying in her bed, the phone held at an angle to capture herself and the naked back of a man who slept next to her. I moved closer to bring the image into focus then sucked in a breath. *Holy shit—that's Shane!* I whipped my gaze back to her. "Does Shane know you took a picture of him sleeping?"

She snatched back the phone, cradling it to her chest. "I'm sick of losing men to you trashy Patten women." The words growled through clenched teeth, and she left my question unanswered.

"What are you talking about?" My hand curled around the

top of my desk chair, needing the stability of anything solid to hang on to because I had a good idea of what she'd meant.

Professor Elian pushed back some of her hair from the side of her face. "Your mom's a whore." An ugly laugh fell from her dry, cracked lips. "I should've known. Like mother like daughter. Shane is the same. He's just like his daddy. Joe was screwing your mom while he was with Cece in college. It was all about who would be the best payout. Your mom wasn't even a contender, but she was fun to party with."

"Uh, who's Cece?"

She snorted. "Shane's mom."

His dad was sleeping with my mom and Shane's. Gross.

"Small world, right?" Cindy cackled. "Gerald Bennett ran Joe out of town once Shane's mama found out what a gold digger he was. And when he came back years later for a fun time at the lake, Katrina wanted to run away with him, but Joe wasn't having that. Not with her stupid, annoying kids. Cece never even knew he was in town." Her laugh was pure evil. "Nor did his boys. But Joe and I understood each other, and that period during his offseason was just like old times. The drugs, the partying, and all the plans we had. It was heaven, until that whore slept with my husband."

"Who?" It was hard following her.

"Katrina." She spat my mom's name. "Keep up. Katrina kept bringing around her little monsters, complaining about what a burden you were."

I sucked in a breath, not liking where she was going. Fear crawled over my body, holding me in place. I couldn't have moved if I wanted to because I had a feeling what came out of her mouth next would turn my world upside down more than she already had.

"Joe told your mom that he had enough brats of his own—even though he had nothing to do with them—and he wasn't taking hers on too." Professor Elian shook her head, tsking. "He and I knew one another from when we were kids in the same hellish group home, later a foster home, and of course, college. We were close. He had my back when I'd needed him. But then I met my meal ticket in college, and he thought he'd found his. We went our separate ways—for a while."

Whoa, Joe married Shane's mom as a con? Did I get that right? Tremors ran through my body as I tried to pay attention to what she was saying, not daring to think too hard about how Summer and I fit into the picture.

"Katrina was my best friend, and she'd been through so much. She was widowed then got herself addicted to drugs—again. We saw Joe a few times in the offseason back then, when he wasn't at the casinos. He promised to take her away with some of that family money he'd gotten his hands on. But that was Joe. Too bad she couldn't see what a liar he was."

That word hit me hard. *Liar.*

Her smirk was pure evil. "Joe needed to score more cash, and Katrina had nothing." Professor Elian's legs buckled, and she caught herself on my bed. She giggled then climbed up and sprawled across my mattress, still keeping me in sight.

Inside, I was a goddammed mess, but I had to keep it together. I wanted to know everything she did, no matter how horrible it was.

"I was a good friend to Trina. She shouldn't have screwed me over."

I shuddered, the nickname my mom went by clicking into place in my memories and pulling forth many unwanted ones—parties, drugs, Summer and me hiding or, if we were lucky, with Mrs. C in her apartment.

"My husband, Tim, was a cheating bastard."

Ironic.

"But when I caught Trina in bed with him, all bets were off." Dark laughter filled the room.

My grip on the back of the desk chair tightened painfully,

but I needed the sensation to ground me in the moment so I wouldn't fall apart from the horror of what she was telling me.

"She talked about how much she hated you both every time we were with Joe, how much better her life would be if you weren't around and she was free. So I did it for her. And me." She bared her teeth. "Just a little revenge for fucking Tim. I pushed you brats into the water. I even jumped in and held one underwater, but you…" She pointed a finger at me, her unfocused eyes narrowing.

My heart thudded against my chest in a desperate beat for freedom. Bile climbed my throat. *I think I'm going to be sick.* I swallowed repeatedly, willing myself to hold it in.

"Somehow, you managed to climb onto my back, and I had to let that other kid go. I got you good, though, with an elbow to your temple. You slid off me then."

I bit back a whimper, my grip on the chair the only thing keeping me on my feet. I vaguely heard a crack. I looked down. It was one of my nails. The pain never came. I doubted I could feel anything else. I was already full of it. *My mom didn't kill my sister. Professor Elian did.*

"You scratched my neck good, and I was afraid the cops would find my skin under your nails, but the lake took care of it, I guess."

"Mom came for us." I barely recognized my voice. *How was I supposed to process that Mom went to prison when it was Professor Elian that was guilty?*

"She was strung out. I knew she wouldn't remember what happened. But by then, Joe was outside. He gave me a look like he used to when we were kids. He had my back. And I knew he was fixing things when he bent to say something in your mom's ear."

My mouth filled with saliva, and I swallowed frantically, feeling horribly sick from the venom spilling from her lips.

"Joe took off. I was glad he got away. I knew we both would be okay. He'd fixed things."

Fixed what? I hung onto her words, even though they sounded far away, like I was back there, underwater.

"I had to swim away, climb farther down the bank, and hide for hours, shivering from the cold water. I got sick, which was your fault. Everything is your fault." Her eyes narrowed to slits. "How did you like that little mind fuck when I called you a killer? The anonymous notes. Did you wonder if you were the one who killed your sister?"

I swayed as images bombarded me. The water. The woman holding Summer beneath the surface. I glimpsed a man laughing on the shore, but I couldn't see his face. Then I was going under, but I managed to grab onto the lady's shirt and climbed her like a spider monkey. I fought, but she was stronger. The horrible sensation of water going down my throat. Breathing it in, panicking. How heavy my body was. Then someone dragging me to shore. I remember vomiting water and coughing so hard it hurt. My sister's eyes. She never responded. I reached for her, needing her, terrified of being alone.

A hazy form filtered through my thoughts of another time, when I saw the faceless man with my mom. The closer he came, the more the shadows receded until I could finally see. It had to be Joe.

I snapped back to my dorm room as anger rolled through Professor Elian's words.

"I'm done with losing men to you trashy Patten women. I made amends. I didn't plan on messing with you when I found out you got into Thane. I could've. One word to the dean would've done it. Who would let you in here with a mama convicted of murder?" Her anger turned menacing, and she growled through her teeth. "But I didn't do all that so you could waltz in and take Shane from me. I killed the wrong girl. And doesn't it fucking figure?"

I was trapped in a nightmare. The information she spewed was challenging to process. But I needed to hear it all and knew there was more. Through numb lips, I forced the question out. "Did you kidnap me?"

She giggled and dropped her head to her arm. "I knew Shane was with you. I snuck into your room after he left and saw that he forgot his wallet. I knew how to get you then."

"How did you get into my room?"

"I have a key. I had to screw the maintenance guy a few times, then I swiped it. I can get into anywhere. Shane always falls asleep after sex, and you sleep like the dead. It was easy. Joe wants money from Shane. He'll get it too. Maybe he'll take me with him when he leaves again." She shrugged. "Maybe not."

A knock sounded at my door, and I fumbled behind me until I felt the handle. When I opened it, Shane stood on the other side.

CHAPTER SEVENTEEN

Seeing who was sprawled on Winter's bed brought a bucketload of dread and remorse. "Why is Cindy in your room?" I'd brought it on—it was my fault, and by the look of things, Cindy had done all the damage she could to Winter.

"Cindy, huh?" Winter's face was pale, but color grew to form deep red slashes across her cheeks. "Well, your 'girlfriend'"—she added air quotes—"did drugs at the lake house with my mom and your dad. They were all there when Summer died."

"You shut your fucking mouth." Cindy launched herself off the bed.

I stepped in front of her, my shoulder blocking her from getting to Winter. She bounced off me and fell back against the bed.

"Stay there." The glare I shot her wouldn't make her stay for long, but it seemed to knock her off track enough. My focus sharpened, and I smelled the alcohol rolling off Cindy and saw the way Winter's features were drawn and pale. It seemed my dad was even more of a piece of work than he'd let on. "What else?"

Tears filled Winter's green eyes, making them shimmer, and

I wanted to take her in my arms, but I needed to be a buffer so Cindy couldn't get to her.

"She confessed to killing my sister."

Holy shit. I hadn't expected that. Something wasn't adding up. *Cindy, Katrina, and Joe partied together at the lake the day Summer drowned?* But Joe had said he hadn't come back until recently. *He lied.* I whirled around, my words more growled then spoken. "What does Joe have to do with you now? With Winter?"

"Everything." Cindy slurred. "Guess who helped me kidnap her?"

I would kill him. "Why was he involved?"

She shrugged, a Cheshire grin curving her lipstick-smeared lips. "That's for him to tell."

Since she was talking, I needed to pump her for information. "Why did you try to frame me?"

"You never should have rejected me. It was just a hint of what could happen if you don't do as you're told."

She was deranged. "Who knew about the wallet?" That part didn't make sense.

"I stole a key."

"Your girlfriend—"

"She's not." I cut Winter off. "I can explain."

"You're mine!" Cindy shrieked, my dismissal seeming to act like a slap to her wounded ego. Then she dragged an oversized shoulder bag toward her that had been on the bed. She unzipped it.

I jerked forward, thinking she was going for a gun. She wasn't. She pulled out Winter's shoebox and dumped it on the bed.

Winter gasped as the letters from her mom spilled all over the place. Cindy's evil fucking laugh mocked me. "Guess where I found these." She jammed a finger in my direction. "In his room."

"How did you get into my room?" The words were out before I registered the shock on Winter's face. I swiveled to her. "I can explain." *Fuck.* I hadn't wanted her to find out that way. Or at all. I'd planned to put them back.

She shook her head, horror filtering through her eyes. "The article."

"Yeah, no." Cindy laughed, glee written plainly on her face. "That stroke of genius was all me." She winked at me. "And getting into your room was easy. You rarely lock your door, and with all those guys coming and going, the front is open more often than not. I just had to sneak in at three in the morning, when I knew you were in this one's room, and boom." She mimicked an explosion with her hands. "I never knew what a jackpot I would find when I searched your room."

I never should have taken them. "Wint—"

"No. I never want to see you again. Or her. Take your murdering fuck buddy and get out of my room." She yanked her phone from her pocket and dialed 911 then hit the button to connect the call. "I want to speak with Detective Carson."

"Winter." I reached for the phone. I just wanted to talk to her, to explain.

She spun away. *Goddammit.* The cops needed to be called. I got that. But with Cindy as drunk as she was, she wasn't going anywhere, and I needed to set things straight with Winter.

Cindy screamed, launching herself into the air and colliding with Winter. The phone flew from Winter's hand. Cindy was a blur of motion I hadn't expected. They went down to the ground. Everything was out of control, spiraling. I had to stop it.

I reached into the mass of hair-pulling and slapping and disentangled Cindy from Winter. "Are you okay?"

"I'm fine, baby." Cindy purred as she clung to me.

"Not you," I snapped. "Winter."

Winter got to her feet and retrieved her phone. When she

looked at me, her green eyes were glacial. "You deserve each other."

It was a verbal slap that I hadn't expected but deserved. I should never have taken her letters. When Winter eventually let me explain, she would see that Cindy was a huge mistake. I had nothing to do with Cindy and hadn't since Winter and I had gotten together.

Sirens sounded too close for me to have time to convince Winter of anything, and I had my hands full trying to keep Cindy from mauling Winter. When the cops showed up at the door, I had Cindy in an impossible-to-move hold. Winter filled the officers in on what had happened. Some of her words were disjointed, but every one she said meant we were finished. I could hear it loud and clear in her voice, and I had never wanted to take back what I'd done more than I did right then.

The cops cuffed Cindy and took her away. Winter had to make a report at the police station and refused to let me go with her.

I left her room with her, following her out before she got in a cop car. "I'll be waiting for you when you get back."

"Don't bother." She didn't even look at me when she said it.

I had to explain, and I wasn't going anywhere until I got the chance.

CHAPTER EIGHTEEN

WINTER

I made my statement at the police station, and an officer drove me back to my dorm. They didn't tell me anything other than that it would be an uphill battle to prosecute Cindy Elian for my sister's murder when my mom was already in jail for the crime, but they would put everything in motion. I was told to go home and try to put it out of my mind. As for Joe Wrenshall, they put out an alert for his arrest and were searching. Once he was found, the case would soon be put to rest.

When I returned to my room, I was worried Shane would be camped out in front of my door. He wasn't, and I was strangely upset and relieved at the same time. But it was good. It was what I wanted.

Isn't it? No. I wanted him there, but I couldn't tell him that. Not yet. What he'd done was wrong, and though he'd tried to explain, I wasn't ready to listen. I needed to figure out some stuff first.

I threw some things in a bag, including the letters, and called Brooke since she was back from Hawaii. I was in no condition to drive, which she detected when I crumbled at the sound of her voice, barely able to get my words out. She freaked and said she was on her way.

Five minutes later, someone pounded at my door.

"Winter. It's me. Open up."

I dragged myself to the door and fell into Jaxon's arms. He shut the door behind him and sank to the floor with me in his arms. My brother held me while I cried and tried to tell him why. I got enough out for him to understand who had killed my sister and kidnapped me.

"I'm going with you," Jaxon said. "Let's go down and wait for Mom. She can stay with you while I pack a bag."

"But you'll miss classes, and what about Max?" Guilt cramped my stomach.

Jaxon flashed that crooked grin of his then popped my nose. "Max will understand. He knows how important you are to me. And I'll email my professors that I have a family emergency. It'll be fine. You need to do the same. Grab your books and art supplies. We can turn stuff in from home this week."

We went outside and waited on the steps for Brooke. When she pulled up, she parked, jumped out, and rushed me. I clung to her for a few minutes until she ushered me into the car. Jaxon took care of my stuff. We stopped at his place, and he ran in and was back in under ten minutes. Then we were on the road. I refused to talk until we got home. I didn't want to make it harder for Brooke to drive.

The drive went by in a blur. My thoughts were in turmoil. I managed to keep it together until we got home. Brooke asked Jaxon to bring everything in, but he already had it in his arms. She gave him a grateful smile and, with an arm wrapped protectively around me, ushered me into the house.

Some tension eased from my exhausted body at the familiarity of the house I'd spent so many happy years in. I went to the living room, grabbed the throw over the back of the couch, and huddled in a corner of the sofa. Brooke and Jaxon followed.

They sat, too, waiting for me to tell them everything. And I did —every detail of what Cindy had said.

When I finished, tears streamed down Brooke's face. She moved next to me and wrapped her arms around me. I rested my head on her shoulder and took slow, measured breaths. Everything inside hurt from what I'd learned.

"I blamed my mom for killing Summer." God, I'd ruined her life. "And while she wasn't perfect, by a long shot, I know she didn't do it. I remember."

"What?" Brooke gasped. "You have your memory back?"

"Yeah. I remember being pushed into the lake and trying to attack Professor Elian. And then nothing until I lay on the ground across from my sister. But the other part I'd forgotten was that Mom had pulled us out. I saw her dragging Summer, then she collapsed near us." She'd been strung out. I'd recognized the signs in her, and when she got that bad, she had huge memory gaps. It had to be why nothing had pointed back to Professor Elian or Joe.

"Your mom going to jail... it's not your fault, Winter." Brooke's hand smoothed my hair from my forehead then ran down my back before repeating the motion.

We spent the evening talking. James came home, and Brooke and Jaxon filled him in so I didn't have to repeat it. His hug was even tighter than Brooke's and lasted almost as long. He, too, reiterated that it wasn't my fault. My mom wasn't blameless about what had happened, and I shouldn't beat myself up.

I understood what they meant. I had told the truth. I remembered Mom there after I was out of the water, but I was a child. Guilt lay in the back of my mind, but it wasn't as much as it should be. And maybe that was okay. So many times, she hadn't fed Summer and me, and she'd said horrible things to us and put us in dangerous situations. She was far from perfect.

Though I felt terribly for my part in Mom's arrest, I couldn't help the relief and freedom I experienced on a daily basis after she was out of my life. Her absence had brought me the greatest gift I could have been given—the Childress family.

I pleaded exhaustion and retreated to my room. It was late anyway. After tossing and turning, I gave up. I couldn't sleep and ended up pulling out the last two stacks of letters, the most current ones, and read through them. I should've done it all at once. I would have known so much earlier. The hate she'd spewed in the first few years had been hard to process. They changed toward the end. Mom hadn't been able to go to Summer's funeral. She'd pleaded for me to visit her, swearing she hadn't killed Summer and would never hurt us. Even as drugged as she'd been, she wouldn't.

It wasn't true. Not only had she hit us, but she had damaged us in other ways.

She mentioned Joe and how she'd wanted to leave us to be with him. A secret part of me was still glad she'd been locked up for as long as she had. I'd gained a real family who had taught me love and showed me they cared in a hundred ways.

I fell asleep with the letters fanned out over the bed. When I woke the following day, they'd been picked up and placed in a neat stack on the nightstand. The scent of coffee was strong. I stretched and sat up to find Brooke sitting at the edge of my bed with two mugs. She smiled, and I offered her one in return.

"How are you feeling?"

I shrugged then accepted the coffee. "Better, I guess."

She gave me a one-armed hug and pressed a kiss to my forehead. "Come downstairs. Jaxon wanted to wait to eat breakfast with you, and he's been a bear because of it the past hour. I held out on making the coffee until a few minutes ago. I haven't told him it's ready yet."

I laughed, and it felt good, natural. "You're making him wait?"

"Of course." Brooke winked.

I got up and washed my face then threw on one of the fluffy

robes I'd gotten for Christmas and went downstairs with my coffee. When I got to the kitchen, I stopped short. The TV was on in the family room, and though I couldn't hear it, I could see my sister's first-grade picture on the screen. I couldn't take my eyes off it.

The story was about how my sister had died and there was new evidence in the case, which they showed with an image of Elian in handcuffs. I didn't catch much, as they were still discussing Elian when Brook hurried to turn off the TV, her face ashen.

"Winter, I'm sorr—"

"It's okay." I would find a way to make peace with it. Maybe not that day, but with the Childress family, I knew it would happen. And to begin, I needed closure. "I think it's time I went to see my mom."

CHAPTER NINETEEN

SHANE

"Did you see the alert from Thane?" Phoenix sat on the couch next to me while Aspen sat outside on their small patio set and worked on a sketch.

"Yeah. Fuck. Everything is just so strange." It'd been a few days since I'd found Cindy in Winter's room, spewing all sorts of shocking shit.

The worst part, for me, anyway, was that I couldn't get ahold of Winter. I'd gone to her room, called, texted, and harassed Piper when I saw her to find out where Winter was and if she was okay. Nothing. Piper had no clue, except that Winter said she would be gone for the week. I didn't like it. Too many misunderstandings stood between us, and I needed to make amends for my part in one of them.

"Isn't that the professor you were sleeping with?" Phoenix hit my shoulder, jolting me from my thoughts.

"Yeah. She was a mistake turned stage-five clinger. Worse actually, more like a stalker."

"What's going on with Winter?"

I'd come clean, filling my brother in about everything. The revenge, finding out what her life had been like when she'd tormented me when we were young. She'd had a reason behind it, and we'd had an invisible pull between us even then. Only, she'd wanted to inflict the same misery on me she'd been drowning in. I understood, and I'd forgiven her. If only she would forgive me too.

"I don't know when she's returning or if she even is. I can only assume she's at her foster family's house."

"She is." Aspen shut the sliding door behind her as she came in from the patio.

Phoenix got up and took her supplies from her. He had her take his spot on the couch and brought over an ottoman for her feet.

She winked at me. "Just think, all I had to do was get knocked up to have your brother wait on me hand and foot."

"Please, I would do it even if you weren't pregnant with our baby." He ruffled her hair, and she swatted his hand away.

"Is Winter okay?" I needed to know.

"She's dealing with things, from what Max has told me. Has she answered any of your calls yet?"

The sympathy in her gaze made me feel even worse. I'd screwed up. Winter hadn't. "No." I'd left so many voicemails and sent more messages than I should have. If she didn't respond soon, I would force Max to tell me where Jaxon's family lived and drive out there.

My phone vibrated, and I snatched it from the cushion beside me. My upper lip lifted in a sneer when I saw who it was —Joe. I held my finger to my mouth, making sure both Aspen and Phoenix took note before answering the call on speaker. My brother deserved to hear what was going on. I was done keeping him in the dark. The secrets hurt everyone around me more than they spared my family—or me—stress.

I wanted to know a few things, which was one of the reasons why I took the call.

"Joe." I gritted my teeth, attempting to stop myself from demanding he tell me what I wanted to know.

"Shane. How are you, son?"

"Good. Just busy with school and working out."

"I wanted to let you know that I have to go out of town but that today would be the day to get me that money. I'll get the paperwork going, and we'll be in business when I get back."

"I can try to get it. Where are you?" I locked eyes with Phoenix, who would let the cops know when we learned Joe's location. There was an alert out for his arrest for his involvement in Winter's abduction.

"Not at the lake house." He chuckled. "But nice try."

Well, fuck. Since he was on to me, I would try a different tactic. "Have you seen the news? I know Cindy Elian, the professor that's being charged with murdering Summer Patten. She told me you were involved too."

"You can't believe her. She was that drug-addicted friend of your mom's."

"She told me something interesting. She said you planned to run away with Katrina Patten using our mom's money." I left out the part about taking Katrina but not the kids. That wasn't what I wanted to get out of him. That would come out in court. Maybe. Probably.

"Your mom didn't have any money. You can't believe that bitch Cindy." His voice held a dangerous note that he must have kept hidden all the times he'd met with me. He sounded backed into a corner and ready to strike. "Forget that woman. She has nothing to do with what we're trying to build. Now, about that money."

"Fuck the money. I'm not giving you a dime. I want nothing to do with you. Don't ever contact me or anyone in my family again."

"You turned out just like your grandfather."

I could hear the sneer in his voice and matched it. "Good. That means I'm nothing like you."

I hung up and tossed my phone across the room.

Phoenix grabbed it out of the air before it could slam against the wall. "He's the same piece of shit he always was."

Anger burned in Phoenix's silver eyes, and I nodded in agreement.

"And on that note," my brother growled, "what is he talking about? What money? What business?"

I closed my eyes and pushed out a breath. *Fuck.* Maybe I shouldn't have put the phone on speaker. "Look, it was a mistake to meet with him the few times I did. When I did, he talked about going into business together flipping houses. He needed a new direction, or career, and wanted something with us."

Phoenix snorted. "What does he really need the money for? I doubt it's for a business with us."

He wasn't wrong there, and it was something I needed to find out. "He'll never get the money. And you were right. We're better off without him." I should've listened to my brother. He'd been right all along. I never should have given someone a second chance who didn't deserve one.

I still believed in them—second chances. I just hoped that Winter did too.

"We had a deal that we would come to one another with problems." Grandad stood on the other side of my door at the football house with Phoenix glowering just as fiercely beside him.

And I hadn't upheld my end of it. He was right, though. I'd sat with him and Phoenix and demanded that he come to us with suspicions, or anything he thought might impact our family, before acting on it behind our backs. I was the one guilty this time. And Phoenix was just as upset with me as Grandad.

I stepped aside to let them into my room at the football house. I'd just returned from grabbing something to eat after hanging out at my brother and Aspen's place.

Grandad must've told Phoenix to meet him at the football house after my brother spilled the beans. I crossed my arms and leaned against the wall. "Let me guess. You're here because of Joe."

"Without going into details, I told you there was more than one reason I didn't want Joe Wrenshall involved in your lives. Do I need to get into the details now?"

"I already know about the trouble he had with the law."

Grandad's eyes narrowed, and Phoenix threw his hands into the air before he fell back onto my bed. He was there in support of Grandad, and I could feel his frustration over the topic of our absent father.

"I already told Grandad, and you, that I didn't want anything to do with Joe," Phoenix said. "I heard him out in his hotel room—"

"Even being around Joe put your brother at risk," Grandad snapped.

"That's not entirely true," Phoenix grumbled. "It was bad timing. I'm on your side about Joe, but don't come down on Shane. In his mind, he was trying to do the right thing by giving Joe a second chance. The only difference is that I refuse to do the same."

My brother had been healing from a TBI, and seeing Joe hadn't helped him that day. It'd made things so much worse. "I never intended to do anything to harm Phoenix. It was just..." A colossal mess. "That day was a mistake. I never should have pressured Phoenix to meet with him. We finally overcame our problems from the summer, and the first semester"—he'd lied to Tracey, and she'd broken up with me, and I hadn't helped him with reading when I knew he was struggling in school—"I don't know. I thought bringing our family together for the first time would be a good thing. When Joe reached out to me, he seemed sincere about wanting a relationship with us, to start over. He even showed us the check you bribed him with that he never cashed. It proved that he didn't want the money, that he wanted his family."

Even as I said it, I found that all the pressure he'd put on me to get him the fifty grand to invest in a business with him told me otherwise. I'd been the one who wanted a chance with someone who was supposed to be a father figure and who was probably the worst example of one.

"The check?" Grandad shook his head, and a low laugh slipped past his lips. "I don't know what bullshit he told you boys, but he cashed that." He whipped out his phone, typed something in it, and hit a few more keys then scrolled before turning the screen toward us.

Phoenix got off the bed and stood by my side.

"This is a copy of the canceled check from the bank." With another swipe, he pulled up a second screen from the same file. "And here is my bank statement showing the withdrawal of that same check."

Anger rolled through me, and I clenched my fists at my sides. He'd put one over on me—Phoenix, too, but he hadn't fooled my brother. He'd convinced me. And the only thing it'd brought any of us were problems.

"He faked the check, then?" Phoenix's head reared back.

"He's a con man." Grandad pocketed his phone. "What he showed you was not the same check. Or the back of it wasn't."

"Well, it doesn't matter anymore." I met Phoenix's silver eyes, and a promise passed between us. We were fully on the same page again, and it was as if a puzzle piece had fit back into place. "I don't want to have anything to do with the man ever again."

CHAPTER TWENTY

WINTER

My gaze bounced around the plain gray walls of the female prison's visiting room. I sat alone at a round table, waiting for a guard to bring my mom out. As I'd requested, Brooke, James, and Jaxon remained in the car. I needed to do it alone, but I would welcome their support afterward.

The steel door with the small window across the room buzzed then clicked open. A guard held it for a rail-thin woman to pass through. She stepped into the visiting room and looked around. I was tense. I knew who she was, and she quickly figured out the same when her gaze locked on me. We didn't smile, and I stayed seated, with the table as a firm barrier between us.

She sat, and a small closemouthed smile curved her lips. "Thank you for coming."

I nodded, unsure about seeing her for the first time in so many years. Her hair, a similar but darker color than mine, was pulled back in a ponytail at her nape, accentuating her high cheekbones and heart-shaped face. What she lacked in laugh lines around her eyes, she made up for with deep grooves bracketing her mouth. Life hadn't been easy for her. It was written in a map on her face and in the hardness of her gaze.

I had no idea what to say to the woman or how to act. The only thing I could do was apologize for possibly being the reason she went to jail. "I'm sorry I accused you of killing Summer. My memory recently came back, and I remember everything."

"You weren't the final nail in my sentencing, Winter. Witnesses saw me pull you and Summer out of the lake. I guess no one noticed Cindy. She probably swam underwater and got out farther down the lake, or that's what I've been told. I wasn't very coherent then, and my memory was skewed. I wasn't even sure I hadn't pushed you both in. Lord knows I wanted to." She said that last part under her breath, but I heard her. She looked away for a moment before facing me again. "I did blame you for a while, but I don't now."

It felt like an apology, and I would accept it as such because I doubted I would get much more out of her. "I was told you wanted to get rid of us, and from most of the things I remember, I could see that as a fact."

She didn't like us. It was something my sister and I instinctively knew.

"I did." She blew out a slow breath. "I loved your father more than anything. He was the one who wanted to have kids, not me. But I would have done anything for him, so I did. He used to say when Summer was born that it was the best summer he'd ever have, and the same with the season you were born in. And while he was alive, he made life bearable. When he was gone, I resented both of you."

I could tell a part of her still did.

"Some people aren't meant to be mothers. I've come to terms with knowing I'm one of them. But it's good to know that at the lake, I tried to protect you and your sister from harm."

"Harm from others but not from what you did to us." The

old hurt and the outrage and sadness surrounding my sister's death remained. A part of me would always blame Katrina, but it wasn't as raw anymore.

She gave a slow nod. "I can see why you would think that."

Her lips pinched together, and anger flared in her eyes. What she'd said to us, that she hadn't fed us at times, and that she'd put us in dangerous situations weren't deemed things to protect us from. I got that loud and clear.

"Why did you write the letters?"

Her dull eyes met mine. "It was part of my counseling program." Her lips curved in a closemouthed half grin. "The last few years of all those nice words made a difference for my parole hearing. Not that it matters, since I'm getting out of here. Nice work on ratting out Cindy."

There was nothing more for me here, and I stood. "Thank you for coming out and meeting with me. I needed to tell you I was sorry for my part in your arrest."

"I'll be out of here soon. And when I am, it's probably best that we go our separate ways."

A weight fell from my shoulders, and a sense of freedom bloomed inside me. "That would be best. I hope you find happiness." And with that, I turned on my heel and left.

I didn't need to know the details about her, Shane's dad, or my art teacher. I'd gotten what I needed, closure, forgiveness on both ends, and freedom to live my life without her wanting to be a part of it.

I paused before pushing through the final door that would take me out of the prison. Not everything was wrapped up in a neat bow yet, though. I'd heard Shane's voicemail confessing his feelings for me. I played it again, just to hear his voice.

"There are things I need to say to you. Leaving you a voice message isn't ideal. It's not what you deserve. But I will tell you one thing now, and I'll repeat it in person so you can see the sincerity for yourself. I love you. I understand that you're going through a lot. I want to be there for you. Please call me back and let me know that you're okay."

I'd had time to digest it and couldn't fight the pull I felt toward him any longer. We needed to talk, to get everything out in the open. That didn't mean I wasn't hurt or angry. I was, and he would hear about it.

It was time to close another door to the past, and I did so by leaving the prison, and my mom, behind.

The best thing about exiting that door, both symbolically and physically, was my family waiting for me. They rushed me, pulled me in for a group hug, and asked me questions to gauge how I'd handled things. We went out to eat then returned home. I would have to go back to school soon. Jaxon left after lunch, as I was out of crisis mode. But I didn't want to head back before having the talk that needed to happen with Shane.

That was how I found myself outside, the phone pressed to my ear as I waited for him to answer. When he did, butterflies took flight in my stomach with a thousand fluttery wings. His deep voice sent a thrill through me, battling against the old hurts, and I smiled. That alone told me it was time for us to talk again.

"Hi, Shane."

"How are you?"

"Better." I knew he could hear it in my voice. "I was hoping we could talk."

"Are you at Thane? Can you meet me at the football house? I'm heading back from lifting now."

"I'm still at Brooke's. I would rather talk here." I gave him the address when he agreed then hung up.

It was a gorgeous day, and I wanted to wait outside for him. Brooke and James had chairs on the front porch, and we loved to sit out there with iced tea or coffee on early mornings on the weekends. It was something I could count on, and they'd caught on quickly how vital those things were to me.

Dressed in a long-sleeved shirt and jeans against the slight chill in the air, I settled in, drawing my knees to my chest, and let my eyes drift shut. I needed the rest after the emotional morning.

"Winter."

My eyes snapped open, and my heart raced when a man's voice cut through the quiet. I knew him. And I should. I'd been drawing him for years, minus the details of his face. But I remembered then, and the man standing before me, trying to act casual, was Joe, Shane's dad.

"Shane sent me to pick you up. He has a surprise for you."

"I don't think so, Joe." I wasn't in the mood for games, and I knew Shane wouldn't want that man anywhere near me.

His eyes hardened, and his lips pressed into a tight line as his hand went around his back. When he brought it forward, he aimed a gun at me. "Get in the car."

"No." I refused to be kidnapped again.

He moved fast and was on me. Yanking me from the chair, he pressed his hand tightly to my mouth, wrenching my arm painfully behind my back. I hadn't even had a second to scream and alert my family.

"Don't do anything stupid. I will shoot you, not to kill but to keep you from going anywhere."

Joe forced me to a vehicle and shoved me into the passenger seat. He kept the gun trained on me as he rounded the front of the car. I slipped my phone from my pocket, hit the redial button, and dropped it between the seat and the door so he wouldn't see it. The driver's-side door opened, and he got in.

When he pulled away from the curb, I started talking. "How did you find me?"

"Cindy was more than willing to share all the details about who my son was involved with."

"Where are you taking me, Joe?" I purposely used his name, but he said nothing. "Fine, why are you doing this, Joe?"

He laughed, but the gun remained in one hand as he steered with the other. "I've got nothing to hide anymore, sweetheart."

Gross.

"I'm going to ransom you to my dumbass kid. He won't get money for his old man, but he will for you."

Wow, we both had winners for parents who loved us so much. *Asshole.* It was just one more thing that Shane and I had in common, and I felt for him. It sucked to find out what a piece of shit a parent was and to have them verbalize their true thoughts of their kids. I kept up the questions, asking things like, "Are you taking me back to where you kidnapped me the first time?" I had to do everything I could to help Shane figure out where I was and send help.

CHAPTER TWENTY-ONE

SHANE

Joe's voice came through the speaker, faint but unmistakable as he confessed his plan to ransom Winter. Backed into a corner like the rat he was, he'd used the only ace he thought he had. Panic had me in a chokehold. I had to do something. I would not let him harm her or win.

My brother and cousins were still in the locker room, getting dressed after lifting. I was almost out the door, having showered in a rush to go to Winter's, but I turned around. I needed their help.

I muted my end of the call so I could hear Joe and Winter talking but they couldn't hear the noise from my end coming through her speaker. I couldn't call the police without ending the call, and the lifeline Winter had given me was too vital to risk that.

Speaker volume on high, I returned to my family. Their conversation tapered off as Joe's voice echoed off the walls. "He has Winter, and I know where he's taking her."

They didn't question me. Just threw on the rest of their clothes and shoes.

"I'm driving," Cole announced.

We followed him, silent as the rolling conversation between Joe and Winter played out. A car door slammed, and scuffling came through the speaker before the call disconnected.

"Fuck!" That terrified me more than when I'd been able to listen in.

The tires squealed as Cole peeled out of the stadium's parking lot, and we sped toward the highway and McMillan Lake.

"I can't believe he's taking her back there," Phoenix said from the back seat. "What an idiot. Doesn't he know that's the first place we would look?"

"Yes." It wasn't surprising. It was where the first crime had taken place.

Damon leaned forward from the seat behind Cole. "The cops have already been there. They wouldn't think to check it again."

"What's the plan?" Phoenix asked.

"One of us needs to record everything. I've had enough problems with being brought in since the incident with Luke. We need to show Joe has Winter against her will, and I don't know if he has a weapon, but she's probably tied up."

"I'll record it."

It was the right move for my brother to be the one to document the events as they unfolded, and I understood why he'd volunteered. He knew I had to be the primary in the confrontation. The recording was a way to take part in hitting Joe where it hurt the most.

"We need to call the cops."

Cole was the voice of reason. I didn't want to. I wanted to take Joe down myself before my hands got tied by the cops getting there. But I couldn't risk Winter's safety.

"Call them. I just hope we get there first. Joe won't do anything until he's got me with the money." Doing something before the cops arrived was a risk but one I was confident would work out. He would be a fool to harm Winter, because that would severely diminish his chance of getting what he wanted: money.

Cole called the cops and put it on speaker. He held it up as Damon leaned forward, ready to help. When it got to the point where we were told to stay away, Damon hit the mute button several times to break up Cole's words: "I can't hear you. Can you repeat that? You're breaking up."

They would have heard, "Can't hear… repeat that… breaking…"

With our end still muted, Damon hit the button to disconnect the call, and Cole turned off the highway for the exit that would take us to McMillan Lake.

We fell silent, the miles dissolving beneath the tires as Cole tested the speed limit. If a cop caught us, we would lead him to the lake house, but I hoped none would.

The tension in the car intensified the closer we got, and my mind raced with every scenario I would soon face and what could go wrong. But one thing kept popping into my head: I needed to call Grandad.

He answered on the second ring. "Grandad. I fucked up, and now someone else is paying the price for it."

"What happened?"

The chill emanating through his voice didn't faze me. We'd been through enough together, especially with how he'd stepped up during my legal troubles. I knew he would be there for me.

I explained about Joe and how we'd met and discussed the business he wanted to start with us. "It never felt right. The money or the urgency. And now I know why." I pushed my hand through my hair, tugging at the strands. "Joe took Winter. He's ransoming her for the fifty grand in cash."

There was a slight pause, then, "And this Winter person, is she important to you?"

"Yes." My voice cracked, and I cleared my throat.

"Tell me where the exchange will happen, and I'll meet you there with the money."

That was family—the willingness to do anything to help the ones we loved. I closed my eyes briefly, forgiving Grandad of all his prior interferences in that one moment. "Thank you. I can't tell you how much that means to me. We're a few minutes from where Winter and Joe are, but I don't think we'll need the money. Phoenix, Cole, and Damon are with me. We'll overpower him."

"Have you called the police?"

"Yes. I think we'll get there first." I hoped we would.

"I'll call Frank and have him go to the police station if you need him. I don't like this, Shane. Joe is unpredictable, and I don't want any of you getting hurt."

"I promise we'll be careful. I'll call you as soon as it's over."

"Do that."

I swiveled in my seat until I could meet my brother's gaze. "I had to call him."

"I know." He nodded. "I'm good with it. Things are better, especially after he apologized to Aspen and explained how he thought he was protecting me."

"After Joe, I can sort of understand."

We were five minutes out when my phone vibrated. I held it up so everyone could see Joe's name on the screen, then I answered and put him on speaker.

"Joe."

"I have your girl." His hated voice filled the silent vehicle.

"What are you talking about?" I couldn't let on that I knew. I could barely contain the urge to reach through the phone and strangle him.

"Winter Patten. The girl you've been fucking." He laughed. "Imagine my surprise when I found out from Cindy. She enjoyed telling me about the two of you."

Guess we were dropping all pretenses. "Stick to the fucking point. What do you want?"

"Fine. Right to business. I'll release the girl for fifty grand."

"It's not at all coincidental that it's the same amount of money you wanted me to put into the flipping-houses scheme you were selling."

"That was never going to happen. Better you know it now."

Especially since you're going down, old man. "Let Winter go. If you do—no harm, no foul, though it's the second time you've kidnapped her."

"Yeah, not a chance. I want my money. You owe me that."

I didn't owe him shit, and he knew it. I needed to keep him talking. At the very least, it would keep him preoccupied and away from Winter. "Why did you take her again? What was the point the first time? There was no ransom demand."

"I fucked up that first one." He chuckled. "She got free. Cindy thought it would be a good-enough lesson to get her to stay away from you, and I wasn't above helping out a friend. Maybe it worked—for Cindy's game. But then again, I hadn't thought I would need the girl to motivate you to get me the goddammed money. Turns out I do. You have an hour to get the fifty grand in cash and bring it to the lake if you ever want to see Winter again."

The line went dead, and I put my phone back in my pocket. "Joe is mine." I needed to reiterate it so they would not interfere when I took him down.

"We'll still be there. We've got your back." My brother offered his support, and my cousins echoed the sentiment.

I cleared my mind of everything but the coming battle. And when we pulled onto the road lining the lakefront houses, I was ready. We parked out of sight and raced through backyards until we found the cabin where Joe was staying.

We crept to the windows, staying hidden in case he was near them. He wouldn't expect me so early or the rest of my family. I peeked through the glass pane. Joe stood with his back to me and a gun in his right hand. He held it pointed at the ground for the time being.

Winter was tied to a chair. I motioned for Cole to hand me his phone then swiped to the camera and hit record, setting it on the windowsill for another angle of what was about to down. Damon would record as I rushed Joe. I motioned for Cole and Phoenix to go around the back then splayed my hand wide twice so they knew to go in on the count of ten.

It didn't take long to reach the front door as I hunched below the window. I doubted the door was unlocked, but I prayed it was. Breaking in the door would give Joe too much time to get the gun up and pointed at me. As I tested the knob, I felt resistance.

I didn't need to look but knew Damon and Phoenix would have their phones in position and already recording. We needed evidence of what happened. I couldn't take any more legal strikes against me.

The countdown finished. I kicked the door, busting in. The crash was loud as the doorframe splintered near the flimsy lock, and Joe whirled around, lifting his gun to point it at me. I lunged, grappling him with a firm hand on his wrist. We went down, smacking hard against the ground with him taking the brunt of the fall.

He fought against my hold as I tightened my grip on his wrist, slamming it repeatedly into the ground. The gun fell from his hand and skated across the wood-planked floor. He shoved me hard, bucking with his hips, and we rolled. Scuffles announced my cousins and brother entering the room.

"Get her out!" I shouted.

I needed to concentrate on Joe and not worry Winter could get hurt. Someone would remove the gun. Then it would be just me and Joe. He wasn't in top shape. I could overpower him, but

I wanted to make it clear who threw the first punch, even if he had the gun.

His fist clipped me across the face. That was what I'd been waiting for. I flipped him on his back, then cocked my arm to slam it into his face. Images bombarded me fast and furious—the single punch to Luke. The thud of his head. I couldn't do it.

I needed to change, and that was the time.

It took everything in me to uncurl my fist and hold him down without beating the hell out of him, but I did it. Just in time too.

The sound of sirens pierced the air, further penetrating the haze that had clouded my sight. I jumped up and stood over Joe. My brother blocked the back exit. Damon the front, and Cole was outside with Winter. No one would let him pass. "You have nowhere to go, so don't even try running."

Dark-gray eyes filled with hatred glared at me before cataloging the position of my brother and cousins. "You would be wise to give me that money and let me go."

I huffed in disbelief. "And why would I do that?" Sarcasm dripped from my question.

"Who do you think I owe the money to?" Joe hauled himself to a sitting position.

I tensed, but he didn't try to lunge for me, at least, not yet.

When I didn't take the bait, he growled out the answer. "The mob, you idiot. What do you think they'll do if they don't get the fifty grand? Or if I'm behind bars?"

So that was how he knew about the connection between the Bennett crime family and the distant familial ties to us. He was in deep with them. "They'll enact their revenge in prison. Or the interest will compound until your release. Either way, it's not my problem."

"It sure as shit is your problem." He tensed at the sound of sirens approaching, his pupils narrowing to pinpricks and his fists clenching by his sides. "They'll go after next of kin, and that's you and your brother."

"No one knows that. And you aren't our father. Not in any of the ways that count. You haven't been in our lives until recently, and I hardly think that'll be on their radar. You're not even listed on our birth certificates." The slight widening of his eyes filled me with satisfaction, knowing how smart Mom had been to do that. "No paper trail will lead back to us."

Not two minutes later, cops swarmed inside. Phoenix stood in the hallway with his camera angled to capture the room. The gun lay under Damon's foot as he recorded from his camera, and Cole's phone still sat in the window.

Joe was hauled out in handcuffs and shoved into the back of a squad car.

"We'll need all of you to come in for questioning," one of the officers said.

Winter's green eyes pleaded with me to stay, so I did. My brother and cousins stayed by the SUV to wait for me. She perched on the edge of the ambulance bed as Debbie, one of the paramedics, checked her for injuries and the forensic photographers took pictures of the bruises on her wrists for evidence. The more Debbie spoke with Winter, the more her stress eased and tension melted from her shoulders.

After wrapping a blood pressure cuff around Winter's arm, Debbie took her vitals. I inched closer, and she reached out, intertwining the fingers of her free hand with mine.

"How are you feeling?" Debbie recorded her blood pressure then tested her temperature by swiping a handheld device across her forehead. "Any pain anywhere?"

"No. Just…" She held up her wrist. "But it's not bad."

Debbie removed the cuff and inspected Winter's wrists, pressing gently. "Does this hurt?" Winter shook her head, repeating her response after each prompt from Debbie. "The bruises will fade, but you can ice them and take some aspirin or

Tylenol if they bother you. Nothing seems to be broken or fractured."

A small smile curved Winter's lips, some color returning to her pale features. "Thank you. Am I free to go?"

"Yes." Debbie helped Winter hop down. "If you notice any other pain that concerns you, go to the ER."

"I will."

We moved to the side, and I handed Winter her phone after one of the cops found it wedged between Joe's passenger seat and the door. "Are you going to call your family?"

"Yes." She leaned into me, and I wrapped my arm around her waist, anchoring her to my side. "Have you called yours?"

"No. My brother or cousins will." I needed to stay with her, and they knew that.

One of the officers approached as Winter pressed the phone to her ear. Tears rolled down her face, and her words were rushed as she talked to her family. She turned into me as the cop grew closer, and he locked his gaze on me, giving her that small amount of privacy.

"We'll need you both to come to the station."

I nodded. "We'll head there from here." I didn't make a move to leave, wanting to give Winter a moment to wrap up her call.

My brother and cousins waited by the SUV as the cops cleared out, giving Winter and me some time alone before we had to go.

She said goodbye to her family, shoved her phone into her pocket, then launched herself into my arms. I held her tight. I never wanted to let her go.

"Thank you for helping me"—she pulled back enough to look at me—"again."

"I'll always be there for you. I'm just so goddammed sorry for everything Joe put you through."

"Shh." She put her finger against my mouth. Then she brushed her lips over mine in a soft caress.

I took control, grazing her bottom lip with my teeth before tracing the seam with my tongue. She gasped, and my mouth slanted over hers, the hunger between us impossible to deny. Her arms wound tighter around my neck, and I pulled her closer, angling her head to deepen the kiss. I was lost in her breathy moan, her responsiveness to my every touch, and how she felt in my arms.

But I'd left some things unsaid, and I reluctantly broke the kiss. Releasing my hold on her so her body slid down mine, I set her feet back on the ground before I led her to the steps. We sat beside one another, and I got ready to pour my heart out. She deserved to know everything.

"We need to talk about some things. This may not be the best time, but I can't go another second with everything between us as it is." I tucked a strand of her hair behind her ear. "I'm not proud of this, but it's something you should know. We have too many secrets between us. You shared yours with me about your mom. Knowing why you treated me the way you did when we were younger helped me come to terms with things in a way nothing else could have. Thank you for that."

She opened her mouth, but I shook my head. I needed another minute to explain.

"When I first saw you having coffee with Piper, I recognized you. I wanted revenge, and I'd planned to make you fall for me so I could discover all your secrets, exploit them, and hurt you in the worst possible way."

Her lips formed an O, her face showing shock but not condemnation. It was a sign that I badly needed.

"The more you opened up to me, the faster I fell for you until it was too late. I did take the letters. It was a spur-of-the-moment thing when I stumbled upon them while tying my shoe. But I knew I had to give them back. I couldn't hurt you. I didn't want to. Not anymore. You're a different person. We both are. I fell for you despite, and maybe because of, our history. I can't imagine a day without you, because this past week has been hell. I miss you, Winter. I hope you can find it in your heart to forgive me. I love you."

Emotion shone brightly in her eyes, and her smile transformed her from gorgeous to stunning as she threaded our fingers together. "I love you too."

CHAPTER TWENTY-TWO

SHANE

I opened Winter's door, and as she climbed out of my SUV, her hand naturally reached for mine. We made our way up the walkway to Mom's house as the sun's rays chased away the lingering pink hue of dawn. It'd taken some convincing for Mom to meet with the girl who had tormented me when I was younger—her words—but we were finally there.

I'd suggested dinner before her shift at the hospital, but the glare I'd gotten told me we needed to start smaller. Instead, we stopped by after Mom's shift.

Worry knitted Winter's brow, and her grip tightened on my hand. Her pale skin seemed to have lost even more color.

"Hey." I tugged her to a stop so she faced me. My hand went to the side of her face, her skin like silk beneath my fingers. "Everything's going to be okay."

I firmly believed that. It wouldn't take long until Winter wrapped my mom around her finger. She just didn't know all of Winter's trauma—but that would change this morning.

Winter's teeth sank into her bottom lip before she released it. "I don't see how it can be okay. Your mom had a front-row seat to what I put you through as a kid. I don't know if any mother—aside from Katrina, maybe—could forgive someone for doing that to her child."

The front door opened before I could respond, and Winter stiffened, her eyes wide. I kissed her forehead then tugged her up the front steps.

"Hey, Mom."

"Shane." Her blue eyes, dark half-moons underneath, were cold as they fell on Winter. She was still in her scrubs, her hair twisted into a messy knot on her head. "It's been a long time since I've seen you, Winter."

She released my hand like it was on fire. "Hello, Mrs. Bennett."

Mom held the door wide and moved to the side so we could enter. I settled my hand on the small of Winter's back, guiding her to the kitchen, and followed the rich aroma of coffee. After pulling out one of the stools, Winter sat at the island where Mom had set out some fruit. Mom followed and took a seat while I poured coffee.

"Mom, do you want any?"

"No. Just water."

I got that, too, then joined them. No one said anything. Mom was furious. I couldn't blame her, but she didn't know what Winter had gone through before we reconnected or what I'd planned to do to her.

"Winter and I are dating." I'd already told my mom, but it was a good icebreaker to start a conversation. I avoided the visual daggers Winter threw my way.

"And you think that's wise? Based on your history?" Mom's voice dripped with ice.

"We're not the same people as we were then." It was a warning for Mom to calm down and listen. What I needed was Winter to interject, to tell her story. And that was as good an introduction as any. I just had to wait for her to take the bait. I didn't have long to wait.

"I don't blame you for questioning my presence in your son's life." Winter turned to face my mom. "I was horrible to Shane." When Mom said nothing, Winter swallowed, took a deep breath, and forged ahead. "He thought I targeted him then because of his stuttering."

"Didn't you?" Mom raised a brow, her lips compressed into a firm line. She was furious.

"It wasn't why, not at first." She cast a nervous glance my way before squaring her shoulders. "I should probably start at the beginning. Shane told me you knew my mom and we were in some playgroup together as kids. I-I don't remember any of that."

"It wasn't long," Mom explained. "I went a few times with my boys, but my schedule wasn't conducive for normal playgroups with other parents and their kids. I know about your father dying. I'm sorry for your loss. Although, that doesn't excuse how you treated my son."

"No. Of course not." Winter clasped her hands together. "Maybe it's because I'd known Shane from the few times we'd met for that playgroup when we were little. I don't know. I felt a connection, a pull when I was around him. I just didn't understand it then. Things were... bad. My mom was terrifying to live with. My sister and I didn't have food all the time. We were in some pretty bad situations, and when I saw what a good life Shane had, I wanted that. Then my sister was killed. I was all alone and in so much pain. My grandparents didn't want me. I was a burden. And Shane... was kind. It only made the pain worse with how I existed." Her lower lip trembled. "I wanted him to feel what I did. It was wrong. I know that, but back then, I couldn't..."

Some of the tension eased from Mom's shoulders, but the lines around her mouth remained.

Winter took a second to regain control of herself. "I used the stuttering as a way to lash out. It was wrong. I don't remember much of what I did or said to him."

It was enough. She didn't need to rehash everything. "Winter didn't know who I was when she transferred the Thane. I recognized her, though. And she's right"—I shifted my focus to Winter and smiled—"something draws us together." I refocused on Mom. "You need to know that this time around, I was the one who went after her. I lied to her, gave her a fake name, and planned to use her."

"Shane," Mom scolded.

Like she didn't know what her sons were capable of. "I didn't end up going through with what I'd planned. I fell for her instead. And Joe—"

"That bastard," Mom growled. Her hand jerked, and some water spilled over the edge of the glass she held.

"Yeah, well, I was guilty of talking to him. I thought if I gave him a chance…" I was getting off track. "It was a mistake, and Winter paid for it."

"At least we found out what happened when Summer was killed." Tears rolled down Winter's face.

Mom turned to her and sucked in a breath. She squeezed Winter's hand, and more of the anger dissipated. That was what I needed to see happen—Mom to view Winter as a person, not a bully who'd messed with her kid.

"I've learned my lesson where Joe is involved. I'll never let him back into my life."

"I'm so sorry, Shane. I wish—"

"Don't. Phoenix and I didn't need a father figure. We had Grandad and Uncle Lucas. We're lucky, and we know it. So don't blame yourself, because there's nothing to feel bad about. He took advantage of you, and I can't believe I'm going to say this, but luckily, Grandad saw through him and got him out of our lives."

Mom laughed then set her water on the island. "Don't ever let him hear that."

"No kidding. Can you imagine the fallout? We'd never be able to reel him back in. Back to me and Winter."

Mom's hand was firmly in Winter's by then. I wasn't sure if she was aware of it. She was a nurturer by nature. Things would be good between them eventually. Some color had returned to Winter's face, which told me she sensed it too.

"Winter and I worked through everything that happened in the past and recently. She has a family that loves her now, and someday soon, we want you all to meet."

Mom's eyes widened, and her gaze darted between us.

"Oh, no. I'm not… we just want the people we love to get to know each other. No other reason." Winter's face turned red.

That time, I did roll my eyes.

Mom's hand fluttered to her chest, and she pushed out a relieved breath. "Okay, not that I would judge you. I'm the last person who would."

"She's not pregnant." I laughed. "Who knew my brother would be the one you had to worry about more than me?"

"Please. You're both trouble." Mom laughed with me then took a deep breath. "So, you're dating. I take it things are serious between you two?"

"Yes."

"We're just dating. I'm not moving into the house with them next year." Winter took a tentative sip of her coffee.

"That's good to know." Mom pursed her lips. "If you two can forgive each other and move forward, then I'll do the same."

"Thank you. I don't deserve you giving me a second chance, but I appreciate it." Winter's green eyes brightened as she blinked the moisture away.

Mom stood then hugged Winter. "I can see how much my son cares about you." She moved back and held her at an arm's length. "We should all"—a yawn hijacked her words, and she covered her mouth, giving into it—"get together for dinner soon."

It was a step in the right direction. My mom was amazing, and I hadn't doubted she would find it in her heart to forgive the girl she'd warned me to stay away from. Even if the morning hadn't gone as well as it did, I would have kept after Mom until the two of them had a good relationship. There was no other option. *Because this girl... she's my future.*

CHAPTER TWENTY-THREE

WINTER

Enough time had gone by that life finally felt settled and as it should be. My mom had been released from prison, and Professor Elian, held without bail, was awaiting trial. She would likely be found guilty and her new address would be the California State Penitentiary. Joe had been arrested for kidnapping, and Shane's lawyer was working to stack more charges against him to lengthen his sentence.

Since my mom had been released, she'd upheld her end of the agreement and hadn't attempted to contact me. That chapter of my life was over. It gave me great relief that she had no interest in rekindling a relationship. I was free.

I didn't have everything figured out, but I knew Shane was a hero, as were his brother and cousins. The press had been all over the story, and we'd had enough of it. Which was why we all decided to go to the cove after our last class of the day.

My lips curved into a smile as I remembered my conversation with Shane that morning.

"Do you want to get coffee after class today?"

"I was going to ask you to move in with me, but coffee sounds good."

Shane was moving into a house with his brother, cousins, and their girlfriends in the fall. Even Aspen and the new baby would be there. I was tempted, but I wanted to take things slow and stay in the dorms one more year. He'd understood. It wouldn't be so bad. I already anticipated sleeping at his place often, and I knew he had the same thought.

Sunlight glistened off the water, and I dipped my toe in. When Shane had suggested we go to the cove with everyone, I was all for it and was glad that Brooke had insisted I learn to swim when I first came to live with her. I'd learned to conquer my fear of swimming, though not of Lake McMillan. Of course, that place represented such pain.

I leaned against Shane's side, and he wrapped his arm around me. Enjoying our afternoon at the cove, we sat with our legs extended past the shore and into the water. We'd jumped from one of the cliff's ledges—not one of the high ones, which we reserved for Riley and Aspen once she had the baby in a matter of weeks—and were drying off in the sunlight.

I loved Damon's and Cole's girlfriends, Riley and Skylar. But Aspen was the one I'd gotten closest to over the past few weeks. I'd been brought into their inner circle and had joined the rotating shift to make sure someone was with Aspen when Phoenix wasn't. Everyone was worried because of the partial bed rest the doctor had put her on with strict instructions not to lift anything heavier than her purse.

We'd bonded over art and had planned some exciting developments together for the future. Jaxon and Max were around often, at the cove that day as well, and I loved every minute I got to spend with my brother and the new family I found in all Shane's people.

But Shane and I had a few things to discuss, and it seemed like the perfect place to do that as we relaxed on beach towels. "What are you going to do about football? Have you decided if it's what you want?"

"I have. Football has been a large part of my life that I've shared with my brother and cousins for so long. I'm not ready to let it go. I want to finish my degree in business management before going into the NFL, so I'll wait until senior year to enter the draft."

I pulled my damp hair over my shoulder, idly twisting the wavy strands around my finger. We'd made our relationship official and exclusive after the incident with Joe at McMillan Lake. Since then, we'd spent every moment we could together, which wasn't easy with classes and football training, even though it was offseason. But we found time, and much of it was spent with his brother, Aspen, and everyone else, including Jaxon, which made me so happy. They were an incredible group of people, and I loved being a part of their world.

But the one who filled that hole inside my heart most was Shane. He didn't know what I'd decided recently, and it was the perfect time to tell him. "I changed my major yesterday."

"You did?"

He lifted me onto his lap so we were facing one another. "You're not getting your bachelor's in fine arts?"

"Not quite. I'll have a dual major in art and psychology. But I want to get my master's in art therapy. I'm still interested in submitting my art to galleries, but I want to work with traumatized kids. That means an additional two years of school and…" I grinned, excitement racing through me. "Aspen and I talked. She loves what I want to do for a living and suggested a fantastic idea."

Shane grinned, and I swore a thousand girls fainted at the sight—or they would have if we were anywhere else. But it wasn't for anyone else. *It's for me.*

"Well, don't keep me in suspense. What was the idea?"

Right. He'd distracted me with his hotness. Mentally, I rolled my eyes at how easily I got sidetracked around him. I expelled a deep breath and let the thrill of future plans with Aspen wash over me again. "Once I'm working with kids and have some candidates who would benefit from surfing or learning how to, she wants to have an arm of her custom surfboard business focus on donations for children's surfboards and lessons. The children would decide if they wanted something they'd done in art therapy with me as the artwork on their board, or they could work with Aspen or me to craft a new design for them."

He cupped my face, understanding swimming through his blue eyes. "We'll make it work. I've already told you that you're it for me, Winter. If staying here is best for you, for us, I can always take over my grandad's business rather than hire an acting CEO while Phoenix and I are away."

"No, I can't let you do that." I should have been shocked, but I wasn't. Not after everything Shane was willing to, and had, risked for me. "Our dreams are important, especially with everything we've endured. We'll work it out. I can do most of my classes and work remotely, and in the offseason, if we can come back here, that would be ideal."

"We can make that happen."

I laughed and flung my arms around his neck. He hugged me tight, and the sense of rightness, and freedom, filled me. That was where I was happiest, with Shane. And from the plans we would continue to share and change as needed, I knew everything would fall into place exactly as it should, with both of us walking hand in hand, partners in a relationship that was meant to be.

WINTER

March

The faint silvery glow from the moon spilled through the blinds that Shane and I had forgotten to shut before we'd fallen into bed last night. I lay there, sprawled across him, and tried to determine what had woken me. It was quiet at—I squinted at the alarm clock's blue glow—three in the morning.

I held still, listening to see if it was something from one of the other rooms or just the weird witching hour that pulled me from sleep. We'd decided to stay in Shane's room at the football house because Piper and her boyfriend were in mine due to something with his roommate. I didn't need the details and hadn't asked.

Shane shifted, his hand sliding over my bare back and settling possessively on my hip. A wave of desire swept through me, and I moved onto an elbow to look at his face. He was so peaceful in his sleep but by no means any less masculine. Power radiated from him. Quiet strength and something else connected us in a way that told me he was mine and I was his. I felt it in my soul and was finally done fighting the pull between us.

My gaze dropped to his lips then lifted to find his eyes open, the pupils dilating, and his features taut with lust. Need clawed at me. He buried a hand in my hair and urged me closer. His mouth captured my lips, and all thought about why I was awake fled.

I clung to his shoulders, the muscles bunching and flexing beneath my fingers. He broke the kiss, his hands everywhere as he trailed kisses down my neck, electric currents following in the wake of his touch. I needed more and ground against him, desperate for the friction he could provide. When his teeth scraped against the sensitive spot where my neck and shoulder met, I moaned, writhing on top of him.

His hands slid down my back and encircled my waist before he lifted me to sit on top of him. We'd gone to bed in only my panties and his formfitting boxer briefs. Still, it was too much between us.

He was long and hard between my thighs. I shifted my hips, rocking against him in a sensual glide, teasing him just as much as myself. The deep rumble from his chest sent a thrill through me, and I arched as his hands trailed over my hips and waist until he finally touched me where I wanted. He kneaded my breasts, and I felt them swell from his caress. When he sat up, his arms snaking around me, he took my nipple in his mouth, swirling his tongue around the tight peak. I cried out.

My fingers tangled in his hair, tugging the strands as another wave of heat rolled through my body. "I need you." The breathy words tumbled from my mouth with a gasp as I ground my hips against him.

He lifted me, tearing my panties from my body. My heart raced as he laid me on the mattress. A second passed, goose bumps running over my skin from the loss of his heat, while he yanked the last barrier of clothing from his body. There was the tear of the condom wrapper, then he was over me, nudging my legs wider as he teased my entrance.

He held there. I tilted my hips, trying to get him to push inside, but he held back. My head tipped into the pillow when he slipped his hand into the slickness between my thighs. He teased and caressed me as I writhed beneath him, whimpering from the intense pleasure.

"Please," I moaned as he pressed against my entrance again. My nails dug into his shoulders in my frantic need for him.

His mouth slanted across mine. At the same time, he thrust deeply, seating himself fully inside me. He pulled out all the way, only to slide back in, and I cried out as every nerve ending in my body was overstimulated in the best way. I trailed my hands over his body, enjoying his sculpted perfection as I met his every thrust.

The deep moan that tore from his throat sent a thrill through me. I gasped as heat built and stars exploded behind my eyes. He drove me wild. Sensations ripped through me, and the orgasm seized my entire body as I tightened around him.

He increased his pace, pumping deep once then twice before he followed me over the edge.

After he disposed of the condom, we lay together, our limbs entangled. He pulled a sheet over us then toyed with the ends of my hair. I was content and secure in his arms. My hand splayed over his chest, enjoying the beat of his heart and wondering if it matched the pace of mine. The sun would be coming up soon, but I didn't want to fall asleep. I tilted my head back, and he turned his face toward me.

"I love you. And I think, in a way, I always have," I said.

A smile played around the edges of his mouth, and his blue eyes sparkled as he cupped the side of my face then feathered over my cheek with the pad of his thumb. "I love you too,

Winter." He tightened his hold on me briefly before we relaxed into the mattress.

It wasn't long before I dozed, only to wake again as the sun crested the horizon, weak rays slanting through the window. I blinked the world back into focus as Shane shifted beneath me, his arm reaching for his phone.

<hr>

Shane

All exhaustion fled as adrenaline coursed through me at the group chat's message lighting up my phone's screen: *Aspen's in labor at the hospital.*

"We've got to go." I lifted Winter off me, gently setting her fully on the bed, and dropped my feet to the floor. "Phoenix and Aspen went to the hospital. She's in labor."

Winter shoved her sexy hair out of her face and hurried after me. We got cleaned up, dressed in record time, and were on the road within twenty minutes. I called Phoenix through the hands-free option and eased the pedal down more so we flew along the highway.

"Are you on your way?"

"Yeah, dipshit. You didn't tell us which hospital."

"Really?" Phoenix growled, but some of the tension eased from his voice, which had been my intent with the insult. "We're at Mom's."

That was all he needed to convey, and I bypassed the exit for the hospital closest to the university. We had another twenty-five minutes to go, but I could probably shave five off that.

"How is Aspen?"

"In a lot of pain and squeezing the hell out of my hand. She isn't talking much. But Mom's here, and that seems to help."

"Of course it does. Our mom is amazing. And does this mean the end of your football career?"

"She's holding my left hand. I gave her my right, and she slapped it away, growling about stupid football players taking unnecessary risks."

"Ah, man. I wish I'd been there. I would've been cheering her on."

"Don't think you're exempt here."

Aspen shouted something in the background.

"What was that?" *Do I really want to know?*

Phoenix laughed. "She said you can come into the room when you get here. She needs another idiot footballer to throw things at."

"Maybe we should send in the girls." I glanced at Winter. "It's probably safer."

"Wait a sec." A muffled sound came through the speaker, his hand probably covering it. "Scratch that. Go to the waiting room for now. She'll want everyone in after." His voice dropped to a whisper. "She's overwhelmed, but the good news is the doc said he doesn't think it'll be long before the baby gets here."

I increased my speed a little more. "Are her parents on the way too?"

"Yeah, I think so. Aspen called her sister, and she relayed everything to their parents." The speaker produced more muffling, then he came back on the line. "I gotta go."

The call disconnected, and Winter's hand settled on my thigh. I grinned as she gave me a tired smile.

"Are you nervous?" Her voice was raspy from the little sleep we'd managed to get.

I had to think about it for a second to pinpoint my emotions. "Maybe a little. I never expected Phoenix to get married and have a baby before me. None of us did. I was the one they were taking bets on." I was the only one who'd been in a serious relationship for years before Phoenix and my cousins found their soulmates.

Traffic picked up as more people got on their ways to work. I adjusted my speed. We were making good time—I had to control the nervous energy pinging inside me.

"Hmm." Winter traced circles on my leg with her finger. "Who do you think will get married next out of the rest? Wait." She turned to me with a wide smile. "Max and Jaxon will. I know it. They're so far gone for each other. Every time we see them, I'm surprised that they don't have a big announcement."

"Really? You think this early?" We were nearing the end of our first year of college. "I could see senior year."

"Oh, right." She fell back against her seat. "I think I've got commitment on the brain lately."

"Hey." I threaded my fingers through hers. "You're not worried about us, are you? Because I'm serious about you. We'll be there one day too."

"No. No. That's not it at all." She pushed her strawberry-blond hair away from her face. "I think it's the uncertainty with the draft, and I know that's not for another three years. Maybe it's not that." She pursed her lips, deep in thought. "I think it's all the changes that happened this year."

"Well, there have been a lot. My brother found out he's going to be a dad. He and Aspen got married. You met everyone in my family, then my estranged sperm donor and your art professor kidnapped you… I would say it's been an eventful year."

"True." She squeezed my hand as I took the exit ramp to the hospital. We would be there in a few minutes.

"Besides, Cole is a year older than the rest of us and going into the draft at the same time as Phoenix. My bet is on him proposing to Riley first."

"We need to go to more of Riley's diving meets. I can't believe how incredible she is."

"We will. And the Olympics." I was damn proud of her, as

was everyone else in our tight group. "Our family will get tickets for you too."

"I can't believe she's going to be in them. It's in two years, right?"

"Yep." I pulled into the hospital parking lot. We fell silent as I found a spot, and as soon as the SUV was off, we were out the doors and hurrying inside. I held Winter's hand as we raced through the hallways, up an elevator, and skidded to a stop in the labor-and-delivery ward. A nurse walked past us and smiled.

"You're Cece's son?"

I nodded, vaguely recognizing her. She had to be one of Mom's coworker friends who had seen Phoenix or me in the hospital either visiting Mom or as patients.

"They're in room 407. I'll let your brother and mom know you're here."

"Thanks." I wanted to follow after her and push my way into the room, but it wasn't the time, and I knew Aspen wanted us to wait until after the baby was born. It wasn't the same as the false alarm last time that'd turned out to be Braxton-Hicks contractions. Then she'd been fine with me being there.

"Hey."

Winter and I turned at Cole's shout.

"Did they have the baby yet?"

The elevator dinged as the doors closed behind him, Riley, Damon, and Sky as they hurried toward us.

"We just got here too," I said.

The nurse returned, her eyes wide as she took in our expanding group. "Cece will be out in a minute. You can all have a seat in the waiting room." She pointed to the end of the hall.

Winter had to tug me to get me to go in the direction the nurse had indicated. I still wanted to barge into the room where my brother and Aspen were, but I let her lead me away. When we were either seated or pacing, Sky and Riley slipped out and returned with coffee for everyone. A few minutes later, Mom joined us, wearing her scrubs, her dark hair secured into a loose bun at the nape of her neck. She looked tired but excited.

"She's doing great. Almost there." She accepted a coffee from Sky and took a sip, her eyes briefly closing as the caffeine did its magic. "I'm going back in, but I suspect the baby will make an appearance in the next hour."

"That's fast, isn't it?" Riley asked.

"Yes. Aspen told us that her mom's labors were very short for her and her sister, and she's in exceptional shape. You guys doing okay?" She stood and kissed my forehead before saying a soft hello to Winter.

It had taken a few visits home for Mom to completely accept Winter into my life. But after that first meeting, when Winter had broken down in tears and apologized for what she'd done as a kid, Mom had melted.

"We're good. Thanks for the update, Aunt Cece." Cole wound an arm around Riley's waist, pulling her close.

Mom hugged my cousins and returned to Aspen's room. We settled in for the duration of her labor. Damon pulled Sky onto his lap, and she curled into him.

"I closed on the house." Cole grinned.

"And we thought, as a surprise to Aspen and Phoenix, we could all pitch in and decorate the room," Riley said as Max and Jaxon burst into the room with armfuls of stuffed animals and balloons.

"What?" Max lost his grip on a plush white teddy bear that would have fallen to the ground if not for Jaxon swooping in and grabbing it. "When is this happening? Because I have ideas."

"What the hell, Max?" Sky straightened, a hand on Damon's chest having helped her push herself upright. "You're making us look bad with all that."

Jaxon rolled his eyes, and the corners of his lips twitched as he fought a grin. "We bought enough for everyone to bring something in."

Cole ran his hand over his face. "I hadn't even thought of getting something for the baby. We were in such a rush to get here."

"You should feel like a jackass," I teased.

"You're the twin. If anyone would look bad, it'd be you," Damon fired off, barely holding back his laughter.

I shrugged. "My brother is conditioned to be disappointed in me. You too." I motioned to Damon, who chuckled.

"Yep. We complained about running all those years and blew it off when we could. So true."

"Not anymore," Cole, the voice of reason, injected.

"Ugh, enough football talk," Sky grumbled and fell back against Damon, her eyes fluttering closed. "The season hasn't even started, and all you guys do is run drills, lift, and watch tape."

Damon kissed the top of her head. "But you love me anyway."

"It's impossible not to." Her words were soft, and she snuggled closer.

I winked at Winter. She'd gotten used to how we teased one another. "See what you'll miss living in the dorms? All this and so much more daily."

"Stop pressuring her." Riley leaned over and smacked the back of my head. "I did the same thing with the dorms."

"But you were never there." Sky snickered.

"It's fine," Winter said. "I'm sure I'll hardly be in the dorms next year, either, but I don't want to move too quickly."

"You're kidding, right?" Jaxon leaned forward in his seat and caught Winter's gaze. "After everything that's happened? Plus, I'll be there with Max. It would be amazing. You'll change your mind."

"All right." I didn't like the thought of anyone pressuring her.

"She'll move in when she's ready. Everyone, back off." I wanted her to live with me when she was ready, not because my family, or hers, twisted her arm.

Everyone fell silent, and I rolled to my feet as my brother entered the waiting room with a wide grin.

"Well?"

"Quinn Bennett is here. She's beautiful, and Aspen is amazing. You guys can come see her now."

I wrapped my brother in a hug, fighting the tears that threatened. "I'm so happy for you, bro."

"Me too. I still can't quite believe I'm a dad. She's so tiny. I just want to protect her from everything."

I laughed because goddamn, it was surreal. "She's going to have the fiercest uncles and aunts."

After I released him and the rest of the crew hugged and congratulated him, we headed toward the room where my mom, Aspen, and baby Quinn were. True to their word, Max and Jaxon passed out the gifts so we each had something to bring into the room.

Crowded inside, our large group fell silent, stunned at the sight of Aspen with a tiny baby cradled in her arms. She looked exhausted and radiant. Happy tears streamed down Mom's cheeks, and I pulled her against my side. It wasn't long before little Quinn was passed around from one of us to the next, stealing hearts with her tiny features and big blue eyes.

"She's so sweet." Winter traced a gentle caress over baby Quinn's cheek.

Strange things were happening to me watching Winter hold my brother's baby, and I rubbed my hand over my heart. I wanted that but with Winter. The whole thing. Marriage, kids, family. Maybe not that day, but seeing her with a baby in her arms solidified our future, one I wasn't sure I could wait until we graduated before I put it into action. But maybe that was okay.

A soft smile curved Winter's lips, and she lifted her gaze to meet mine. A wave of love so strong hit me at the sight of my thoughts mirrored in her green eyes. No matter where we ended up after the draft and with her career as an art therapist, I knew we would have everything we ever wanted.

BONUS EPILOGUE

SHANE

Five Years Later

Shrieks and laughter mingled with the calls of the California gulls as they took to the sky, scattered by two blond toddlers on a mission. When four-year-old Quinn and two-year-old Hadley got too far from our group, Phoenix took off down the shore and scooped them up in his arms. He twirled them around to a chorus of giggles. I'd never seen my brother so happy. He and Aspen were expecting their third child. She was in her first trimester, as was Sky, who had just found out she and Damon were expecting their first.

I lowered myself into one of the chairs we'd brought to the beach then rolled my shoulder to ease the ache. We were all in recovery mode, as the season had ended for California only a month after my Texas team lost the Super Bowl to Phoenix and Cole. But we always had next year, and if our quarterback stayed healthy, then our chances increased for victory, unlike that February.

It was hard to believe Damon and I had entered the draft only two years ago. He'd gone in the sixth round to Washington, just after Texas had taken me as a fifth-round pick. We were happy. Sky loved Washington and worked for the *Washington Post*. But with their first child on the way, she planned to quit, possibly write a book.

Cole dropped into the chair beside me, running his hands through his dark hair before kicking his legs out in front of him. I handed him a water. It was offseason, but we maintained a strict diet and exercise regimen to stay in peak shape.

"Where's Riley?"

It was ten in the morning, and our entire clan was at the beach, minus Max and Jaxon, who were due to arrive in an hour, as were our parents and Grandad. We were having our weekly barbecue since we were all in the same state until training camp came around in four months.

Cole took a swig of water. "She's sleeping in."

"That's not like her." Riley was an early riser like the rest of us and usually trained first thing. Cole even had an Olympic-sized pool and diving boards on his property so she didn't have to go elsewhere to dive if she didn't want to. We all had gone to watch the Olympics, where Riley had won her first gold medal —her first of what we knew would be many more to come.

"Yeah. I know. I'll go check on her in a few minutes."

I didn't like the worry lines around his mouth. We'd known Riles since she and her mom moved to town while we were in high school, and it wasn't like her to sleep in.

Four dots appeared down the coast, snagging my attention. "Looks like Damon and the boys are on their way back."

Cole grinned. "I don't know who I feel sorrier for, your three boys or Damon for skipping our run this morning."

"Damon. Hand's down. He should've gotten his ass out of bed when you and Phoenix texted. I don't feel even a little sorry for him."

"Why didn't the boys go out with us this morning?"

Winter and I had fostered Tyler, Matt, and John, three boys who were in a group home and had been labeled as difficult and unlikely to be adopted. They were two years apart in age ranging from ten to fourteen. Since neither of us had been easy at that age, and after meeting them, we knew they belonged with us. Winter's dream was to adopt since she had come out with such a positive experience and loving family after being dumped into foster care at a young age. She knew trauma, and when we went back to see if there was a little girl to add to our brood, we met Daniela, or Dani, as she preferred. Her tragic story had left her with internal scars, something Winter was a godsend at helping her work through. As was Brooke, Winter's foster Mom.

It had taken a handful of months to bring Dani out of her shell, and we would keep her in counseling for as long as necessary. Winter did art therapy with her and the boys, but the light at the end of the tunnel had been when our twins were born. Dani had fallen in love with River and Ivy. They were the spitting images of us. River's dark hair and blue eyes were like mine, and Ivy, a daddy's girl—I loved every minute of her sweet attention—had Winter's bright-green eyes and strawberry-blond hair.

My heart warmed as I visually trailed the three building an elaborate drip sandcastle together as they barely stayed out of the waves that broke along the shore. It wouldn't last. River, the little instigator, was a mini terror. He would stomp on it, and Ivy's temper would ignite. Those two were best friends and mortal enemies.

Phoenix set down his two girls by Dani, River, and Ivy. Aspen and Winter joined them, and by my son's hand gestures, an elaborate sandcastle city would soon be born. I wouldn't be surprised if River grew to be an architect someday. He was forever building things, and his special awareness at such a young age was remarkable. Maybe. *Who knows?* I wasn't worried. Whatever my kids wanted to do, I would support them wholeheartedly.

Sand sprayed my legs, and I tore my gaze from the kids. "Watch it."

"Fuck off." Damon dropped into a chair, his chest heaving. "Tyler is going to be a track star."

Cole laughed. "Serves you right for skipping this morning."

"He had you sprinting the entire way, didn't he?" I asked.

Ty loved to run, and he did so as if someone were chasing him.

"He needs to do sprints with us next week."

"Now you're talking." Cole tapped my water with his before tossing Damon one.

The first year with the boys, all brothers we didn't want to separate, had been rough. But nothing they did fazed Winter or me. When Dani had come into our household six months before the twins were born, things had begun to settle into a routine. It helped that we had a virtual village to raise the kids. And while I loved being on the Dallas team, my agent kept feelers out for any trade possibilities to California. It was hard on the kids to move to Dallas during the season and then, in the offseason, back to California. We'd done it that year, but we wouldn't be able to for long, not with the older kids in school and sports. It wasn't fair to them.

"Did Matt and John keep up with you guys?"

John wasn't a fan of running. Not like Ty and Matt, who were more athletically inclined. Matt, and possibly Ty, enjoyed throwing a football or playing scrimmages and running routes with the rest of us. John, the oldest at fourteen, had taken to Grandad, as he worked at the property management company part-time when we were home. He had a head for business. But structure was vital, and we ensured they were all included in activities and kept busy. Because of that and the unconditional love we gave them, no matter what attitude they threw at us, they flourished.

When Winter had shared her story with them about growing up with an abusive and drug-addicted mother, her sister's death, the abandonment, and her stint in foster care—then having Brooke, James, and Jaxon take her in and becoming a real family—their resistance to us had melted away, mostly. We still had tough times, but we handled them with consistency and love.

Damon downed the rest of the water and grabbed one of the towels to wipe the sweat from his face. "No. John trailed behind, but Matt kept pace with him. I had to match mine to the Flash." He glared at me. "You're going with him tomorrow."

Sky jogged up the beach and dropped into Damon's lap, her arms winding around his neck as he pulled her close.

His hand settled on her still-flat stomach. "How are you feeling?"

"Good."

He tucked a few strands of her long, dark hair behind her ear as Winter joined us. I jolted forward, snaking my arm around her waist, and pulled her onto my lap as she laughed. I would never tire of that sound. I pressed kisses to her neck, and she sank into my embrace, her back to my chest. Her hands settled on top of mine, resting over her stomach. We didn't plan on having more children, at least not naturally. I had a feeling she would want to adopt another kid or two in a few years, and I was okay with that. We had enough love and help with our growing brood to accommodate as many as she wanted to bring into our circle.

"Aspen's ultrasound is in a month." She kept her gaze on the twins. Aspen had joined Phoenix, and her head bent to her girls as they pushed sand to form another castle.

"Are they gonna find out what they're having?" Riley had snuck up on us, and Cole got to his feet with stark worry.

"Are you okay? You slept a long time. I planned to come check on you in a minute."

"Yeah. I'm good." But she seemed distracted as she leaned into Cole's side, her gaze locked onto Sky. "Is Aspen going to find out the sex?"

Sky grinned, her dark-blue eyes sparkling. "She's worried about twins."

The slight color in Riley's face drained away. "Oh. I didn't think about that."

"That's it. We're going to the doctor." Cole tugged on her hand, pulling her toward their house.

Riley's beach bag slipped from her shoulder, but she caught the straps in her hand before it dropped and spilled over the sand. "No, wait." Then she bent and withdrew something, her back to the rest of us.

Cole wrapped his arms around her waist and lifted her as laughter spilled from her lips.

"Really?" he asked.

"Yeah."

"Cryptic, guys," Damon said. "Fill us in."

We had to wait until Cole finished kissing his wife—yeah, that'd happened too. We'd all married our girls—best decisions ever.

When they came up for air, Riley glanced over her shoulder at us. "We're having a baby."

"Congratulations!" The three of us yelled, getting to our feet and taking turns hugging them. We attracted everyone's attention, and the rest of our crew joined in for another round of hugs and excited congrats when they found out.

River tucked his head, pumped his arms, and trucked up the sand with Ivy—who was holding Dani's hand—not far behind. My son barreled into my legs and demanded, "Juice!"

"Daddy." Ivy caught up, tugged her hand free of Dani's, and shoved her brother. "Up."

River bared his teeth and slammed his hands into Ivy. She fell on the sand. Not even a second later, two spots of red colored her cheeks, and she got to her feet then launched herself at her brother with a primal shriek. Her hands fisted his hair, and they rolled. I tried not to laugh as Winter and I separated our warring toddlers. We knew we would be in trouble when the twins started walking at eight months. River went from crawling to running, and Ivy wasn't far behind him. With Ivy in my arms, I calmed her down. Winter scooped up a juice cup and handed it to River, who calmed instantly.

When my son finished his drink, Ty took him from Winter, and the boys went back to the sandcastles, Quinn and Hadley not far behind. Phoenix and Aspen's girls loved the three oldest boys, who doted on the younger girls.

"Everyone will be here soon." Winter's arm went around Dani, who leaned into her side. "We're going to head up to prep the food."

"Okay, do you want help?" I offered.

Aspen snorted. "You guys only get in the way in the kitchen."

"And you eat the fruits and veggies as fast as we cut them up," Riley teased.

"We've got this." Sky kissed Damon then joined the girls. "Girls only in the kitchen."

"Me too!" Ivy lunged forward, her arms outstretched.

We were familiar with the move, and I had a firm hold on her until Dani grinned and took her from me. My girls loved to be included with their mom, aunts, and grandmothers.

I kissed Winter's lips then Ivy's and Dani's foreheads before they followed Aspen, Riley, and Sky as they headed up to Cole and Riley's house. We all had oceanfront homes, thanks to Grandad, who had purchased the land when we were little. He'd thought ahead and had included property for Cole and Damon too. It was his gift to each of us when we graduated college or, in Phoenix's case, got drafted to California's NFL team.

We each built our dream homes, which were always open to our family and had become the hub for gatherings. Each of us took turns hosting our weekend barbecues.

It was also a way for Grandad to keep us near him and our mom. Things had mended between Grandad and the four of us as well as Uncle Lucas. It was the kids that did it. As soon as Quinn was born, they were putty in her cute little hands, and I wouldn't have it any other way.

———

Winter

After the sun hand gone down and we were all in our respective homes, with our kids passed out in their rooms, I climbed into bed with Shane. He closed the book he was reading and set it on the nightstand.

"Sexiest thing ever," I murmured before snuggling against him.

He laughed. "Reading?"

"Mm-hmm." It was hot. I couldn't help it. "There's something about a gorgeous guy reading that's so sexy."

"Any guy?" His brows furrowed as he frowned, which made me laugh.

"Please." I rolled my eyes. "I only have eyes for you."

He moved fast, before I could say anything else, pulling me under him. Then he slanted his mouth over mine. I moaned, my hands sliding up his chest, enjoying how the muscles bunched and flexed beneath my fingers. Then I threaded my fingers in his hair.

When he inched the cami I'd put on before bed up to trail his fingers over my skin, I slid my hands to his shoulders and pushed. His hand stayed beneath the cotton shirt, just above the waistband of my sleep shorts. The slightest touch from him and my body ignited, but I had something to tell him before falling under his spell.

"I want to talk for a few minutes first."

"Is everything okay?" He sat up, leaned against the headboard, and lifted me so I straddled him.

"Yeah, everything is perfect." I flattened my hands on his bare chest, my body warring with my mind. I wanted him, but I had something important to say. "I have a surprise."

His mouth curved into a sexy grin, and I rocked my hips forward, unable to resist him. He was hard and ready for me. He always was.

"Not that kind of surprise." I laughed, knowing his mind was firmly on sex. *Later...* because my thoughts kept drifting there, too, but I wanted to tell him while we were alone. "I got us tickets to Hawaii."

"Nice." He threaded his fingers through my hair, and I sighed into his touch. I loved it when he played with my hair.

"I don't think you're getting it. I have tickets for *us*."

"Not the kids?" His blue eyes locked on mine in surprise.

We hadn't gone away together, alone, in so long. It was time. The kids were doing great, and between my family and his, we had plenty of help. "We'll fly there Friday, spend two amazing days by ourselves, then everyone—"

"Everyone?"

"Yep." I grinned because we didn't travel lightly. Our extended family, including our kids, would take the jet and join us. "What do you think?"

"That you're amazing and I can't wait until Friday." He cupped the side of my face, his thumb brushing back and forth over my bottom lip. "I love you."

My heart swelled. "I love you too."

I leaned in to his touch, little jolts of electricity dancing over my skin from how he affected me. Then he kissed me, and I lost myself to the pull of the man who held my heart in his powerful and capable hands.

The End

Keep up with Isla's releases by joining her newsletter:
https://bit.ly/IslaVaughnNewsletter

If you enjoyed reading WICKED GAMES as much as I did writing it, I hope you'll consider leaving a review.

ACKNOWLEDGMENTS

Thank you to all the incredible readers and bloggers who love this series as much as I do. It's tough to see it coming to an end. It's not really because there will be more! Maybe not with this angsty bunch, but new stories that I hope bring you just as much enjoyment. I'm hoping to get something new to you soon. If you're not already on it, join my newsletter for updates on news and upcoming releases.

I have amazing critique partners whose opinions and creative input I value deeply. Thank you

Emily Albright, Kristin Kisska, Candace Irvin, and Jessica Riley Miller. I'm thankful to have them in my inner circle.

I'm grateful to have Colleen Noyes with Itsy Bitsy Book Bits and Cass Thomasson with Chaotic Creatives in my corner, working their magic to make each release successful.

TE Black Designs knocked it out of the park with the covers for this series. The editors on all of the Hidden Valley Elite books from Red Adept Editing are fantastic and easy to work with. I'm so grateful to have such an amazing team.

Thank you.

ABOUT THE AUTHOR

Isla Vaughn is the author of the Hidden Valley Elite series. Her romance books are full of complex characters, strong alpha males, and the fierce women who bring them to their knees. When not writing, she can be found daydreaming about owning a beach house, reading, or drinking too much coffee.

You can find her at:
https://www.islavaughnauthor.com

Subscribe to Isla's newsletter for cover reveals, book announcements, and giveaways:
https://bit.ly/IslaVaughnNewsletter

facebook.com/author.IslaVaughn
instagram.com/islavaughnauthor
bookbub.com/profile/isla-vaughn
goodreads.com/islavaughn_author
tiktok.com/@islavaughnauthor

ALSO BY ISLA VAUGHN

Hidden Valley Elite Series

Savage Start

Savage Lies

Savage Truth

Brutal Days

Brutal Nights

Cruel Start

Cruel Hate

Cruel Love

Wicked Games

Wicked Ends